Juliet's Story

Juliet's Story

WILLIAM TREVOR

Illustrated by Robin Bell Corfield

RED FOX

A Red Fox Book

Published by Random House Children's Books
20 Vauxhall Bridge Road, London SW1V 2SA

A division of The Random House Group Ltd
London Melbourne Sydney Auckland
Johannesburg and agencies throughout the world

1 3 5 7 9 10 8 6 4 2

First published in Great Britain by The Bodley Head Children's Books 1992

This Red Fox edition 2001

Printed bound in Great Britain by Cox and Wyman Ltd, Reading, Berkshire

Papers used by The Random House Group Ltd are natural, recyclable products
made from wood grown in sustainable forests. The manufacturing processes conform
to the environmental regulations of the country of origin.

THE RANDOM HOUSE GROUP Limited Reg. No. 954009
www.randomhouse.co.uk

ISBN 0 09 941773 1

Paddy Old's folktales have been
told in Ireland for many generations.
Acknowledgements are due to the storytellers
who have kept them alive, and to those who
later collected them.

CHAPTER 1

Often when she couldn't go to sleep, Juliet thought of all the things she disliked most, and all the things she liked. Mashed turnips she hated, and the white of a boiled egg, and seed cake, and the screeching noise her friend Kitty Ann could make by scraping the lid of a polish tin on the shiny surface of her back doorstep.

She liked the banana cake Kitty Ann's mother made, and the little corner of peppered bacon her father slipped on to her plate at breakfast-time was delicious. So was raspberry ripple with hot raspberry jam poured over it, and lime sherbets that exploded in your mouth, and chives chopped very fine and sprinkled over two slices of cucumber on crusty bread. And just as much as anything you could eat she liked lying in the sunshine in Dandelion Meadow, gossiping with Kitty Ann while Kitty Ann's black-and-white spaniel, Madra, slept with his nose laid out on his paws.

Something else Juliet particularly liked was going to the pantomime – once a year, on St Stephen's Day. Kitty Ann went too and there was a drive of nearly fifty miles, which Kitty Ann never minded but Juliet did because if she talked she felt sick. 'Now, Juliet, be careful,' her mother would warn, looking over her shoulder when the whispering in the back of the car began. Her father would remind her that if they had to stop by the roadside they'd miss the first bit of the show.

But, feeling sick or not, it was worth it. The dancers turned cartwheels and swayed with their arms on one another's shoulders. Dick Whittington – or Jack, or Aladdin – was always a lady dressed up, and sometimes there was a Buttons, or giants with legs so long that everyone gasped. Nearly always there was a Wicked Baron or someone else who was wicked, and a Good Fairy. Afterwards you felt in a daze, with the tunes of the songs still in your mind, and Kitty Ann saying it was the best ever, which she said every year. They sat in the Stella Café, her mother and father and Kitty Ann and herself, talking about it, her father telling some of the jokes all over again, and Kitty Ann saying she intended to go on the stage when she grew up. Then the waitress brought them a plate of thinly sliced bread, already buttered, and iced cakes and tea. The best part of Christmas, Juliet's mother said, and for the next few days Juliet and Kitty Ann would practise turning cartwheels and swaying with their hands on one another's shoulders.

When she couldn't go to sleep, Juliet would think of the first moment when the curtain went up, and afterwards in the Stella Café, but she would always end up saying to herself that what she liked best of all in the world was listening to stories. The pantomimes were stories of course – how the birds ate the crumbs the Babes in the Wood had dropped, how the wolf disguised himself in the grandmother's nightdress, the pumpkin and the mice becoming the carriage and the horses, and the slipper fitting perfectly on to Cinderella's foot. But somehow they were not the same as stories you listened to.

Kitty Ann loved Bugs Bunny on the television, and so did Juliet, though not as much as Kitty Ann did. You could *see* Bugs Bunny just as you could *see* the lady dressed up as Dick Whittington: the little television screen was like a picture-frame and at the pantomime there was a picture-frame too, filled up for you with colours and people and things happening. When you listened to stories you had to fill it up for yourself, and that was what Juliet liked. You had to choose the colours yourself, and give the people faces. You had to imagine a seashore or a garden, or a huge factory where the machinery never stopped, which made millions of Snow Whites and millions of dwarfs, and when you pulled down a lever out came millions of ordinary tables and chairs instead, or beds for dolls or chocolate bars. Juliet tried to explain all this to Kitty Ann, but Kitty Ann just said she preferred Bugs Bunny.

Paddy Old told Juliet stories. The first time he told her one she was out for a Sunday walk with her father and Paddy Old said something about the weather and then he began about a Man Who Swallowed a Mouse. What the man had to do was to sleep with a piece of roasted bacon on a plate beside his mouth and the mouse would smell it and come out for it. Then the cat could pounce.

'Why's he called Paddy Old?' Juliet asked when she and her father walked on. Juliet had plaits and glasses, both of which she particularly disliked and did not intend to have when she grew up. 'Paddy Old's a funny kind of name,' she said.

'It is, all right, but I never heard him called

anything else.'

'Is he very old?'

'Maybe nearly a hundred.'

Paddy Old had watery eyes and a shrivelled face, like a walnut in a pickle jar. He had a little white hair and there were always a few white bristles on his chin that his razor had missed, which Juliet imagined was due to his extreme old age. He was always dressed the same: in a black suit with a waistcoat, a striped shirt without a collar, fastened with a collar-stud at the neck. It was because of extreme old age, Juliet guessed also, that he forgot to put a collar on, but when she suggested that to her father he disagreed. He said that it was maybe because Paddy Old liked to be comfortable.

When it was fine and warm enough, Juliet and Kitty Ann would sit on the bench outside Paddy Old's house and he would stand in the doorway, half leaning against it and half leaning on his stick. In winter they would sit by the fire in his kitchen and he would stand by the window. He always liked to tell a story standing up: that was a peculiarity with him, he said, for there weren't many storytellers in Ireland – or anywhere else – who had that preference. 'We're all made different,' he used to say.

Sometimes, when they were outside, Kitty Ann's

Paddy Old had watery eyes and a shrivelled face, like a walnut in a pickle jar.

toe would poke about on the ground, making a
pattern in the dust while she listened. And at
the fireside she would occasionally reach out to
rearrange the turfs. But Juliet never moved. She
listened, enthralled, to the story of the Sailor and
the Rat and the story of the Man Who Lost his
Shadow. Vividly she could see the Frog That Was
a Fairy, and the Cow That Ate the Piper.

'Everyone has a story,' Paddy Old said, 'but once
upon a time there was a man who had none at
all. Rory his name was. His wife used to knit
stockings and he would travel about the country
endeavouring to sell them. Well, one time he called
in at a house for a night's lodgings, and the old man
inside said he was welcome. "Sit down," said the
old man, and as soon as he spoke a chair moved
closer to the fire and Rory sat on it. "Rory and
myself need our supper," said the old man, even
though there was no one but the two of them in
the kitchen. As soon as he spoke a knife and fork
flew up from the dresser and cut down a piece of
ham that was hanging from a beam. A saucepan
filled itself with water and sat down on the fire,
and the next thing was, the ham was boiling in it. A
tablecloth spread itself out, and the potatoes washed
themselves. "Well, now," said the old man when
the meal was eaten, "will you sing me a song?"

But Rory didn't possess a voice that was fit for singing. "Well," said the old man, "in that case tell me a story." But Rory hadn't a story to tell. "In that case," said the old man, "you can spend the night out on the roadside." So Rory picked up his bagful of stockings and went out from the house.

'He walked along the road and met a man who was roasting a joint of beef on a spit. "Would you turn the spit for me?" enquired the man, and Rory said he would. The man went away and as soon as Rory put his hand on the spit the joint of beef spoke to him. "Don't let me burn whatever you do," said the beef, and Rory was terrified out of his wits to hear a piece of meat talking on a lonesome road in the middle of the night. He let go the spit and ran away as fast as he could, but the spit ran after him, hitting him until he was covered from head to toe with blood. The spit left him alone then and Rory hammered on the door of the first house he came to, which was the same house he'd been in before. The old man opened the door and asked him what the matter was. So Rory told him what had happened and the old man said, "If you'd had a story like that to tell me you wouldn't have been turned out. Come inside and rest yourself on the bed." So Rory lay down and went to sleep, but when he woke up in the morning he was lying by the roadside with his bagful of stockings for a pillow and no sign of a house in any direction.'

'Weird,' said Kitty Ann when she and Juliet were walking home together, and she started on about a new programme on television.

Kitty Ann was exactly the same age as Juliet but prettier, so Juliet considered. And although Kitty Ann always shook her head when Juliet said so, Juliet knew that she thought so too. Kitty Ann had curly fair hair and an upturned nose and bright eyes that were the same blue as the blue of a bird's egg Juliet had once seen in a nest.

Juliet lived at one end of the town, in the house next to the old gasworks; Kitty Ann above her parents' shop, Macnamara's Provisions and Bar. Every morning Juliet waited outside Macnamara's Provisions and Bar so that she and Kitty Ann could walk on to school together. She had to wait because Kitty Ann was never in time for anything, but she didn't mind because she knew she was always a bit early herself. On the journey to school they told one another anything that had happened since yesterday, but sometimes if they had poetry to learn, or spellings, they would hear one another instead. They swung their school-cases and always giggled when the Russian Princess called out to them from the courthouse steps in the queer language that nobody in the town understood. It was Juliet who said she was a Russian Princess. Other people said she was a tinker who had been disowned by the tinkers because the language she spoke was one she'd invented herself in order to be contrary. She lived in a rusty old van that had been abandoned beside a tumbled-down house on the Tipperary road.

'That's nothing only rubbish,' Declan Flynn used to say whenever he heard Juliet mentioning a Russian Princess. 'If there's one person in this town that talks rubbish it's yourself.'

Declan Flynn was in the same class as Juliet and Kitty Ann, a fat, black-haired boy who said he intended to become a boxer.

'All flab!' Juliet and Kitty Ann used to shout across South Main Street at him in singsong voices. 'All Declan'll ever fight is the flab!'

Sometimes he chased them, but he had never once caught them because they were good at dodging round the parked cars, down Ha'penny Lane and through the broken grating into the cellars of O'Brien's bakery. They knew every inch of the town – the ins and outs of the ruins at the top of steep Castle Hill, Fitzpatrick's timber mills and the high stone warehouses that ran along by the river. They knew the hiding place under Lawlor's Bridge, where you had to be careful and couldn't rush to in a hurry, and all the places in the old graveyard and among the agricultural machinery and bales of wire at the Co-op. They knew by heart the inscription on the big stone memorial to the 1798 Rising in the square, and what it said above the doorway of P.J. Kelly's hotel: *P.J. Kelly, licensed to sell tobacco and intoxicating liquors.*

It wasn't a big town, but sizeable enough for County Tipperary, Juliet's father used to say. There were three banks, two churches, twenty-three public houses, seven sweetshops, three butchers', a post-office, a supermarket, and shops that sold groceries, clothes, hardware and electrical goods. In a shop that didn't sell anything, as far as Juliet and Kitty Ann could see, there was always a horse-race on the television, and men standing around in an excited state. Fennel's garage smelt of oil, and sometimes you could see petrol fumes coming from the pumps in the sunlight. The brass plates at the better end of the town were engraved with the names of solicitors and doctors. Paddy Old lived at the other end, in one of a row of whitewashed cottages, most of which weren't occupied any more and had grass growing on their roofs. When you looked up from any of the streets, or from the square, you could see the

Galtee Mountains towering over everything. They cut the town down to size.

'Once upon a time,' Paddy Old said, 'there were three brothers – Conal, Donal and Taig.'

Conal and Donal and Taig had an argument regarding a field. Each of the three said he owned it and each claim was as good as the next. So they went to a wise judge to see if the matter could be settled, and the judge said he would award the field to whichever of the brothers was the laziest.

'That's me,' says Conal, 'and no mistake. For if I was lying down in the middle of the road and there was a regiment of soldiers coming at me on their horses, I wouldn't stir I'm so lazy.'

'If I was sitting by the fire,' says Donal, 'and you piled as much turf and wood as you could find on to it, I'd sit there until the marrow would run boiling out of my bones. I'm as lazy as that.'

'If I was lying on my back, on the floor,' says Taig, 'and if soot was falling as thick as hail on me, I would be too lazy even to close my eyes.'

'Well,' says the judge, 'it's still hard to choose. Tell me, though, which of you is the oldest?'

But when the three brothers competed again the judge still couldn't choose, so he asked them which had the longest memory. And when he still couldn't choose he tried for which had the keenest sight, and after that for which of them was the supplest.

'If you filled that field out there with hares,' says Conal, 'and put a dog in the middle of them and then tied one of my legs to my back, I wouldn't let one of the hares out.'

'If you filled that castle over there with feathers,' says Donal, 'on the stormiest day of the year when the wind was blowing a gale through the windows, I would not let a feather blow out.'

'If you stood me on a road,' says Taig, 'I could shoe the fastest race-horse in the world when he went galloping by, driving in a nail every time he lifted a foot.'

Still the judge could not choose, so he tried for the cleverest of the three.

'I'm so clever,' says Conal, 'that I would make a perfect suit of clothes for a man without knowing any of his measurements, only knowing the colour of his hair.'

'As for me,' says Donal, 'I would make a perfect suit for a man knowing no more about him except that I heard him cough.'

'As for me,' says Taig, 'if I was a judge and was too stupid to decide a case that came up before me, I'd be clever enough to give a decision or else we'd be going on all day.'

'If you filled that castle over there with feathers,' says Donal . . .

'Taig,' says the judge, 'you get the field.'

At school there were other stories in the reading book, but they all had to do with pronouncing difficult names, like Alcmene and Eurystheus and Deianeira, Diomedes and Cerynitia. The adventures of Jimeen helped you to learn Irish. Sometimes in a history lesson there was something good.

Paddy Old told the ancient folktales of Ireland, and at home Juliet's mother told her about the Little Mermaid and the Mad Hatter's Tea Party and the Sleeping Beauty. Her father did his best, making up stories about hedgehogs and weasels and stoats.

'Come back to my place,' Kitty Ann always invited after she and Juliet had visited Paddy Old. Her mother, Mrs Macnamara, was a big good-natured woman who was always serving in the shop at that time of day and usually gave Juliet and Kitty Ann a couple of biscuits on their way through it. Mrs Macnamara never minded how much television Kitty Ann watched, but often as Juliet sat there with her friend she found that the pictures she had carried away from Paddy Old's cottage were more real and more vivid than those that flickered on the screen.

Then, one April day, Paddy Old wasn't outside his cottage although the day was warm and fine.

The door wouldn't open when Juliet and Kitty Ann tried it. No smoke came out of the chimney.

'Let's go back and watch Star Trek,' Kitty Ann suggested, which they did. But all through the programme Juliet kept frowning to herself, knowing that something was wrong.

'Wash your hands and sit down at the table,' her mother said when she was back in her own house, and Juliet knew from the quiet tone of her mother's voice that she should be quiet also.

'I'm afraid we have very sad news for you,' her father said.

CHAPTER 2

Everyone went to Paddy Old's funeral because he had lived in the town before anyone else was born. People joined in the procession to the church, walking in a long line that became longer all the time. The shopkeepers closed their shops for a few minutes and people pulled down their blinds while the procession went by.

Juliet and Kitty Ann walked with Sister Catherine from the convent, and afterwards Sister Catherine told them that once upon a time, when Paddy Old was young, he had travelled the length and breadth of County Tipperary telling stories in return for a night's lodging. That was how he had lived. He would arrive at a farmhouse or a cottage and he would stand by the fireside after supper and

They even waited while the grave-diggers reached for their shovels.

tell his stories till the small hours. Or he would arrive in a town and people would congregate to hear him. He walked wherever he went, but in the end he couldn't make such long journeys, so a schoolmaster who had been in the town at that time arranged for him to live in a cottage nobody wanted.

At the very head of the funeral procession the Russian Princess walked, bowing and smiling at the closed shops. The Russian Princess was always there at funerals, taking up an important position, as though she had been the dead person's closest friend.

Juliet and Kitty Ann remained at the funeral until the end. Most people had drifted off by then, having to get back to their businesses. But Juliet and Kitty Ann watched the coffin slipping down into the ground, controlled by the grave-diggers' straps. They couldn't quite hear what Father Quinn said then, but they saw the handful of earth thrown on to the coffin top, and even waited while the grave-diggers reached for their shovels.

'Star Trek's on now,' Kitty Ann said, extra jaunty because she hadn't been able to smile or raise her voice for more than half an hour.

Juliet didn't say anything. The Russian Princess was begging among the remains of the crowd, and a few people gave her coppers.

'Back to my house, Ju?' Kitty Ann invited, but Juliet said no.

After that everything was difficult for Juliet. Although she and Kitty Ann did almost everything together she had often gone on her own to Paddy Old's cottage, and both he and she had known that Kitty Ann didn't appreciate the stories in the same way as she did. Kitty Ann tagged along, just as she tagged along herself when Kitty Ann wanted to watch the timber being sawn at the timber mills or scaffolding being put up at some house that needed repairs. Kitty Ann could stand for ages while the metal poles were joined together and the planks put into place, the workmen shouting to one another, delighted with themselves. Juliet found it a bit boring.

So it was natural that she should miss the stories more than Kitty Ann did. She missed the old man's voice and the way he stood up very straight in the doorway of his cottage or by the turf fire. She missed the look that always came into his watery eyes, a faraway look as if he, too, could see all the people he told her about.

'What's the matter, Juliet?' Miss Walsh at school asked.

'Nothing. Nothing's the matter.'

'Something is, Juliet.'

But Juliet just shook her head.

'As cross as two sticks,' she heard her mother saying to her father when she shouldn't have been listening. 'Very tiresome.'

Her father sighed so loudly that Juliet could hear him through the crack of the door.

'It's the age,' he said.

'What is, for heaven's sake?'

'The way she's gone broody. She's at a tricky age.'

'It'll be years before she gets to the tricky age. I should know. I was a girl myself.'

'Yes, dear,' Juliet's father agreed soothingly.

Juliet knew she was as cross as two sticks. She was cross and she was sulky. She didn't want to answer Miss Walsh's questions even though everyone agreed that Miss Walsh was kindness itself. Her sadness made her cross. It weighed upon her. In all her life she had never felt so sorrowful. She tried to tell herself the stories Paddy Old had told her, but it didn't work properly. The people in them were no better than shadows – the Piper the Cow Ate, the Man Who Lost His Shadow, and all the others. She kept hearing the handful of clay clattering on the coffin top.

'Come and watch Tom and Jerry, Ju,' Kitty Ann invited.

'My name's Juliet.'

'Come and watch Tom and Jerry, Juliet.'

'Tom and Jerry's rubbish.'

'Oh, hoity-blooming-toity!'

Kitty Ann only said hoity-blooming-toity to girls she didn't like. She'd never said it to Juliet before.

'I'm out with you, Julie-blooming-et. So don't try addressing me.'

'I don't want to address you. I don't want to have anything to do with you.'

'Suits me.'

Kitty Ann, red-faced, walked away, leaving Juliet standing outside Phelan's clothes shop in South Main Street.

'Sure, everyone has to die at that age,' Declan Flynn said, finding her alone there.

He was stupid, Juliet thought, standing there in front of her, not leaving her room to pass him by on the pavement. His big head was at an angle, his dull eyes looked down at hers.

'Oh, go away,' Juliet said.

She pushed by him, and when the Russian Princess called out in her peculiar language from the courthouse steps Juliet didn't reply.

'What she needs is a change,' Juliet's father said.

'A firm hand, more like.'

'It isn't nice for you, putting up with her.' Her father shook his head sympathetically. 'Especially at a time like this.'

Juliet could see through the crack in the door. Her mother was fanning herself with a newspaper even though it wasn't hot. Her mother was going to have another baby, a fact that interested Kitty Ann greatly, but as far as Juliet was concerned only meant that her mother wasn't as slender and agile as she used to be, and that she often sat down wearily. Her father paid her more attention than he usually did, which meant he paid Juliet less. The way both of them were now made everything even more difficult. It complicated the sorrowful feeling that was weighing Juliet down and making her cross. 'Taking out of herself,' her father said, 'is clearly what she needs. We could perhaps kill two birds with one stone.'

'Her birthday . . .'

'That should help too.'

They would get her a puppy for her birthday because they knew she wanted a puppy to go around with, like Kitty Ann went around with Madra. A puppy would take her out of herself – a smooth black-and-white puppy without a name, so that she could choose a name herself. Delia she would call it.

'We're going to have a visitor,' her father said on the day before her birthday, and she imagined the smooth little dog on the kitchen floor, sniffing about because everywhere was new.

'Your Grandmamma's coming,' her father said.

Juliet wanted to be cross because her grandmother wasn't anything like as good as a puppy, but it was hard to be cross because she liked her grandmother. Her grandmother's visits always stirred things up.

'Oh,' she said, doing her best to sound casual. 'Is she coming because of my birthday?'

'Nothing to do with your birthday,' her father replied in the voice he reserved for making sure Juliet wasn't getting above herself. 'For another reason entirely, madam.'

'What reason's that?'

'Ask no questions and if you're lucky you'll be told.'

Her father had a way of saying that when she wanted to know something. An irritating habit, Juliet considered.

'I only asked *one* question.' Sitting on the kitchen windowsill, Juliet swung her legs and made the clicking noise in her throat no one else could make.

'I haven't been told *anything* yet.'

'No, you haven't,' her father agreed.

Juliet's grandmother liked to be called Grand-mamma, which was considered unusual. 'I am not a goat, you know,' she used to say. '"Nanna" does not suit an old lady who is not a goat. Grandmamma *if* you please.'

So Grandmamma she was – tall and beautiful, or so Juliet considered. Old, of course, but then – as her Grandmamma pointed out – being old and being beautiful sometimes go hand in hand. And of course she was nothing like as old as Paddy Old had been.

'Happy birthday, Juliet!' she said on the morning of the birthday, but didn't give her a present because, she said, that was coming later.

Juliet got all sorts of things for her birthday, but nothing that was alive, not even a tortoise. There was a box of puzzles, and a kaleidoscope, and a dolls' first-aid kit, and a bird that flapped its wings when you wound it up. There was a card from Kitty Ann even though they still weren't friends. *Love, Kitty Ann* it said in Mrs Macnamara's handwriting, disguised to look like Kitty Ann's.

'Well, off tomorrow!' Juliet's grandmother said.

Juliet had just drawn in her breath in order to

blow it out again at the scarlet candles on her cake. Two of the candles flickered but none of them went out. Juliet looked at her Grandmamma with her mouth open.

'You're not going away again?' she said.

'We're both going away,' her Grandmamma replied. 'As a matter of fact.'

'Who's both?'

'You and me.'

Juliet looked at her father, who was smiling and nodding; and at her mother, who was smiling and nodding also. They said, together:

'Grandmamma's taking you on a little holiday, Juliet.'

'Where're we going?'

'Oh, all over the place,' her Grandmamma replied vaguely, holding out her plate for a slice of cake.

So Juliet packed everything into a blue suitcase her mother lent her – all her washing things and her nightdress, and extra clothes and her hairbrush, and the bird that flapped its wings when you wound it up. Her mother hugged her goodbye and told her to be good. Her father said they'd miss the train if they dawdled.

'Don't forget to bring her back with you,' he

reminded Juliet's Grandmamma at the railway station. 'We only have the one Juliet.'

He laughed to show he was making a joke and Juliet's Grandmamma laughed. She promised she'd do her best not to lose Juliet, who kissed her father, telling him he was silly. Just for a moment she wanted to cry because she knew she'd been sulky and not very nice, and now she was going to miss him.

'Big girl now,' he said, and then the train came in. A moment later he was waving at them from the platform.

The train was the Dublin train, but after that Juliet still did not know where she and her Grandmamma were going. 'We'll take the boat,' was all her Grandmamma had said. 'Flying's for the birds.'

The train passed through hills and woods and boglands, leaving the great mountains of County Tipperary behind. The ticket collector came along and punched their tickets. He said they were having a nice bit of weather. His sweetpeas would be good this year, he said, and Juliet's Grandmamma agreed. Juliet wondered how they knew.

'Now, Juliet,' her Grandmamma said. 'How are you going to entertain me?'

'Entertain you?'

'Well, make the time pass quickly. You know the kind of thing.'

'We could play a guessing game.'

'We *could*. You could run after the ticket collector and all three of us could play a guessing game, since guessing games are better with three. But actually it might be more fun if I told you a story.'

'*Can* you tell stories?'

'Well, I can try. I dare say I'm not much good, but I can try.'

So Juliet's Grandmamma told the story of the Sunflowers in the Snow, which took place in a town that seemed to Juliet to be very like the town she lived in. And while her grandmother told the story it seemed to Juliet that although it was about a boy called Dom it was also about herself. For the first time in her life she felt she was a boy, and that she was *this* boy, that all the thoughts he had were her thoughts, and all he said she might be saying herself.

The way her grandmother told the story was quite different from the way Paddy Old had told his stories. Although she had listened entranced to the adventures of Conal and Donal and Taig, and the Man who Swallowed the Mouse, and the Frog That Was a Fairy, Juliet had never once imagined that she was any of them. 'There are no two storytellers the same,' Paddy Old had said, and listening to her grandmother's voice Juliet for the first time understood that.

In the town that was so like Juliet's town a really fantastic thing happened: some sunflowers bloomed in December.

It was a few days before Christmas and there were four inches of snow on the ground. 'The sunflowers imagine it's August,' said the people of the town. They didn't know what to think.

'Well?' said Dom, a red-haired boy, to Mr Cranley the butcher.

'I haven't seen them yet,' said Mr Cranley. 'I'll go up one of these days.'

Dom wondered about that. He wondered about Mr Cranley, for he knew that Mr Cranley must know more than most people about the sunflowers. Mr Cranley placed his two hands on his butcher's block and looked down at Dom. He said:

'You can't understand everything, Dom. It would be a dull old world if you could.'

Mr Cranley was the only person in the town whom Dom had ever told his favourite secret to. One day, a year or so ago, he had explained to Mr Cranley about how he used to look out of his bedroom window, watching the people and the sparrows.

Sometimes Mr McCarthy, the ironmonger, would pass by, taking his dog Bonzo for a walk on a lead, and when that happened Dom would quickly close his eyes and see everything differently. What he saw was Bonzo taking Mr McCarthy for a walk on a lead, and this always made Dom laugh and laugh.

Sometimes, when he looked across the street and saw Mrs Kilty feeding the sparrows on her windowsill, Dom would close his eyes and see the sparrows feeding Mrs Kilty. And when Danny Fowler, the milkman, drove up the street with his horse and cart, Dom would close his eyes and see Danny Fowler dragging the cart, while Trot, the horse, delivered the milk bottles. That made Dom laugh so much that his mother would shout up to him to stop at once or there'd be trouble. His mother used to say it was his red hair that made him so excitable.

When Dom told Mr Cranley all that, Mr Cranley said: 'You have a Special Gift, Dom. Like someone might have a Special Gift and be able to play beautiful music on a piano or a violin. Or be able to run faster than anyone else. Nobody understands why some people can do things and other people can't.'

'Have you a Special Gift, Mr Cranley?' Dom

asked, but Mr Cranley didn't reply to that question.

He was a large, sad man with an extremely red face, who was very honest and always told the truth. He was always getting angry in the presence of his customers. He would strike his butcher's block with his chopper and complain about the meat that was being produced these days. 'Look at this horrible liver,' Mr Cranley would cry. 'And those revolting kidneys. Meat isn't what it used to be.'

Now, of course, the more Mr Cranley made such remarks about his own meat the more the people of the town refused to buy it, until in the end nobody came to Mr Cranley's shop at all. They used to have to get on a bus and go to another butcher in a town four miles away, which is a long way to have to go for a piece of meat.

From his bedroom window or when he was out and about Dom had watched most of the people in the town, and he had come to the conclusion that Mr Cranley was by far the most interesting.

For one thing, Mr Cranley was always alone. He never went out with a dog or a horse so that Dom could change the two about like he did with Mr McCarthy and Danny Fowler. Once he watched Mr Cranley chopping up some bones, and he closed his eyes and tried to imagine that the bones were chopping up Mr Cranley, but it didn't work. He hadn't expected it to work because he had guessed that Mr Cranley wasn't like other people. He began to watch Mr Cranley very closely indeed. He followed him when he went for walks.

The day after the sunflowers bloomed in the snow, Mr Cranley put on his big black overcoat and walked to the edge of the town to see for himself. It was a particularly cold day and the cold got into Mr Cranley's ears and hurt them, making Mr Cranley sadder than ever. He said to himself that it was a sorry enough thing to be a butcher without customers but to be a butcher with painful ears as well was just about the limit.

While Mr Cranley was thinking this a bus passed him by on the road, and the bus driver hooted his horn. Mr Cranley looked up and waved, but nobody waved back, because the bus was full of mothers and children on their way to the other town to buy meat for Christmas, and they didn't at all care for the sight of Mr Cranley idling by the roadside. A tear rolled from Mr Cranley's right eye, down his large red cheek, and dropped on to the snow.

Just then a car pulled up beside him and two important-looking men got out and marched towards the sunflowers.

A tear rolled from Mr Cranley's right eye, down his large red cheek, and dropped on to the snow.

Mr Cranley watched them. They poked at the flowers. They smelled them and felt their petals between their thumbs and forefingers. One of them scooped the snow away from the root of a plant and cut through the hard earth with a penknife to get a look at the root itself.

When they'd finished all that, the men walked back to the car very slowly. They were talking in quiet voices as they approached Mr Cranley, and Mr Cranley said:

'Good afternoon, gentlemen.'

'Yes,' said one of the men in a rather rude way, not paying much attention to Mr Cranley.

'I'm the local butcher,' explained Mr Cranley, thinking that the men might be impressed by that. He added, because he couldn't help it: 'Meat isn't what it used to be.'

'Yes,' said the same man, in the same way, and whispered something to his friend. They seemed amused by the sight of Mr Cranley with his red face and his big black overcoat.

'What do you think of those sunflowers?' said Mr Cranley. 'Is it a miracle?'

The men laughed. Miracles, they informed Mr Cranley, were a thing of the past. One laughed more loudly than the other. 'You'll be telling us the fairies planted them next,' he said.

Mr Cranley laughed too. 'No, no,' he said. 'We're very modern here, you know. We don't at all believe in fairies.'

Now, during all this time – from the moment Mr Cranley had stopped by the sunflowers and felt the pain in his ears – Dom had been hiding behind a tree. He had seen the busload of mothers and children go by, he had seen Mr Cranley wave at them, he had seen the tear on Mr Cranley's cheek, he had seen the car stop and the two important-looking men get out.

He could hear what they were saying and what Mr Cranley was saying, and he was very interested because he had his own idea about why the sunflowers had bloomed in December.

'There is a scientific explanation for those sunflowers,' Dom heard one of the men say. 'They can't just come there at the wrong time of year.'

'You'd think the cold would kill them,' remarked Mr Cranley.

The men laughed. 'That's just the point,' they said.

Dom watched the men climb into their car and drive away. He watched Mr Cranley stand for a while by the roadside looking after the car. Dom imagined that Mr Cranley was thinking that the men might at least have offered him a lift back to his shop. He watched the butcher heave a big sigh and set off on his own along the snowy road.

Dom knew that Mr Cranley knew something about the sunflowers because one day, a few months before, he had seen Mr Cranley planting the seeds.

Dom slipped from behind the tree and followed Mr Cranley along the road. He walked slowly, taking care to be ready to dart away if Mr Cranley should look round, because he knew that Mr Cranley wouldn't care to find himself being followed. But Mr Cranley didn't look round and Dom followed him all the way to his butcher's shop, where there was one old chop and a half-pound of sausages hanging in the window. Mr Cranley entered the shop and looked about him at all the emptiness. He looked through the window and saw Dom lurking outside.

'I've seen the sunflowers,' he shouted through the glass. 'I think they'll die after Christmas.'

Then he bolted the door and went upstairs.

Dom watched for a little while longer. He saw the light go on in Mr Cranley's bedroom and he guessed that although it was only half-past three in the afternoon Mr Cranley would probably go to bed and read the newspaper because he couldn't think of anything else to do. It made Dom sad to think of poor Mr Cranley in bed with a newspaper, with no wife to talk to and no children to cheer him up. It made him sad when he thought that if Mr Cranley hadn't been so honest he would be a successful butcher instead of one whom nobody could be bothered with. 'Why ever did he plant the sunflower seeds?' said Dom to himself. 'What on earth sort of a strange man is this?'

The next day lots and lots of other important-looking men arrived in the town. They were scientists, and reporters from the newspapers, and people from the television. The hotel, P.J. Kelly's, was packed on every floor, and the twenty-three public houses in the town had to take in some of the visitors.

The television cameras took pictures of the sunflowers so that everyone in the world could see what sunflowers in the December snow looked like, and all the scientists disagreed about why they were in bloom.

Mr Kelly, of P.J. Kelly's hotel, appeared on television in his striped blue suit. He said he couldn't understand the sunflowers standing up to the weather like that. He added, though, that it was good for business.

In the middle of that same night – it was the night before Christmas Eve – Mr Cranley disappeared.

When the morning came, his butcher's shop didn't open and the only person who noticed this fact was Dom. He peeped through the window and could see nothing except the old chop and the half-pound of sausages. All Mr Cranley's choppers and knives and saws were gone and the butcher's block was scrubbed and dry.

'Mr Cranley has gone away,' said Dom to one of the newspaper reporters. 'It was Mr Cranley who planted the sunflower seeds in August.'

'What's this, son?' said the newspaper reporter, taking a pipe out of his mouth.

The police came and opened up Mr Cranley's shop to see if Mr Cranley was still in bed maybe. They thought he might be ill, and although he was a bad butcher they were quite prepared to help him. But Mr Cranley was gone. His clothes were gone. His one suitcase was gone. 'So that's the end of Mr Cranley,' said the people of the town.

'What's this red-haired youngster saying?' asked all the scientists, having heard about Dom's story.

They all came round to Dom's house and Dom's mother made them cups of tea, and Dom told them why the sunflowers had bloomed in December.

'Mr Cranley had a Special Gift,' said Dom, 'which he wouldn't talk about. It's something you get given.'

The scientists sipped their hot tea and smiled.

'There must be a scientific reason for the sun-flowers,' said the scientists. 'You can't get away from that.'

'I have a Special Gift,' said Dom. 'I can close my eyes and change things round.'

The scientists began to talk among themselves. 'So this funny old butcher put in sunflower seeds in August and they flowered in December,' they said. 'We're no closer to the truth than that.'

'We are! We are!' cried Dom. 'I know about Mr Cranley. I watched him. He's not like other people. He has –'

'A Special Gift,' said one of the scientists, and all the others laughed.

Dom became so angry then, jumping up and down and stamping his feet on the floor, that his mother had to tell him to stop or there'd be trouble. So he calmed down.

'Mr Cranley has gone away,' he said, 'to use his Special Gift somewhere else.'

The scientists nodded their heads. They didn't at all believe that Mr Cranley had a Special Gift.

'In the old days,' said Dom, 'wizards had a Special Gift. That was why people were afraid of them. Nobody knows why some people can do things and other people can't.'

'Look here, laddie,' said one of the scientists, 'no one could have a gift like you say Mr Cranley has.'

'Why not?' said Dom.

'Because never in the history of the world,' replied the scientist, 'has anyone been able to arrange for sunflowers to appear all of a sudden through four inches of snow.'

'That is because no one ever had that Special Gift before. You can't understand everything.'

The scientists smiled. 'We think we can,' they said quietly, 'if we try hard enough.'

'No, you can't,' cried Dom, jumping up and down again. 'Mr Cranley said you can't understand everything. He said it would be a dull old world if you could.'

'Now, now,' said the scientists.

'It's his red hair that makes him do it,' said Dom's mother, and she shook her head crossly at him when the scientists weren't looking.

'The flowers are there for Christmas,' said Dom. 'After Christmas they will die.'

The scientists all shook their heads. 'We don't know that, laddie,' the one who had called him laddie before said. 'We don't know that at all.'

'Well, I do,' said Dom.

'How do you know?' asked the scientists

all together.

'Because Mr Cranley told me.'

On the day after Christmas Day the sunflowers wilted and died. The scientists were amazed.

'How did the old butcher know?' they said to one another.

They looked for Mr Cranley but they could not find him.

In the end they packed their suitcases and left the town, with everything about the sunflowers written down in their notebooks.

'Well?' said Dom, seeing them going off.

'Goodbye, Dom,' said the scientists.

'You can't understand everything,' said Dom. 'Now, can you?'

The scientists didn't reply. They looked at their watches and said the train was late.

'Well?' said Dom.

One of the scientists blew his nose. The others stared seriously at the ground.

'It would be a dull old world if you could,' said Dom.

The scientists didn't say anything.

CHAPTER 3

While the story about the sunflowers was being told the train passed through eight railway stations and stopped at four of them. A few people got off the train each time it stopped, and a few people got on. Each time the guard blew his whistle and waved his green flag.

'Aren't you looking great?' a man greeted Juliet's Grandmamma in Dublin, hurrying up to her on the platform of a station that was bigger and noisier than all the other ones put together.

'Oh, so there you are!' Juliet's Grandmamma said.

He was a big man in a tweed coat and hat. Juliet thought he had the look of a walrus because he had that kind of moustache. But he was very kind. He carried the suitcases and then drove them in his car right through the middle of Dublin. Several times he told Juliet's Grandmamma that she was looking great.

'Don't you think so?' he said to Juliet, and before she could reply her Grandmamma told the man to get on with himself.

Juliet thought it was very clever the way he was able to steer his car through all the bicycles and other cars, and people crossing the streets. Wild horses wouldn't get him to drive a car in Dublin, her father said.

'Well, that's the city for you,' the man said when they'd left all the traffic behind. 'Dublin's fair city. Though not as fair as a certain party I could name.'

He turned his head to smile at Juliet's Grandmamma as he spoke, and Juliet thought the car was going to run into the back of a bus that had stopped to pick up passengers.

'Keep your eye on the road,' Juliet's Grandmamma warned.

Juliet could see mountains in the distance and thought it funny that they'd come all this way to be in the mountains, since there were much higher ones in County Tipperary. But she didn't say anything because it would have been rude. Then the car turned off to the left and quite suddenly they were in a harbour.

'The child's starving,' her Grandmamma said in her scolding voice.

'Oh, apologies, I'm sure.' The car drew up at a café, where Juliet had cold beef and fried potatoes with lettuce and tomato, and a peach melba. Her Grandmamma and the man drank Ballygowan water and two cups of coffee each.

'Give her a seasick pill,' the man advised, and Juliet's Grandmamma produced a little white pill from silver-paper wrapping.

'You guessed correctly,' she informed Juliet. 'We're going on a ship.'

Juliet hadn't guessed anything of the sort, so she just smiled and swallowed the pill, washing it down with Ballygowan water.

'Would you ever think she was a grandmother?' the man remarked to the waitress when he was paying the bill, and Juliet's grandmother told him he was disgraceful, discussing her with a waitress.

'Ah, sure, you're lovely!' The man laughed, squeezing her elbow. He winked at Juliet.

'For heaven's sake!' protested Juliet's Grandmamma, red in the face.

'You're great when you're flurried. Still and all, we mustn't spend all night here. Isn't that right, Juliet?'

Juliet said she supposed it was.

They left the café. Her Grandmamma's friend said it was a shame he wasn't going with them, and her Grandmamma told him not to be talking nonsense.

'Hurry up now,' she urged, and then everything happened quickly.

The car moved off. Juliet saw the black side of the ship. The man with the moustache said goodbye to them.

'Go up that gangplank,' a sailor called out, and they went where he directed, carrying their suitcases.

'We'll find somewhere to sit,' Juliet's Grandmamma said.

'Here,' Juliet suggested, pointing at a table with seats on either side of it.

'Perfection!' said her Grandmamma.

They left some of their things there so that no one else would sit in their seats while they were having a look round the ship. There was a restaurant and a shop, and then they found another restaurant and another shop, and a bar and a café. They went up on to the deck and walked from one end of the ship to the other. It was cold and a wind was blowing, but Juliet didn't mind. She'd never felt so excited.

It was better than going to a party.

'Of course it is,' her Grandmamma agreed.

Then the ship began to move and Juliet's Grandmamma suggested that they should return to their seats.

'Wherever are we going?' Juliet asked.

'Wales,' her Grandmamma said. 'Where the witches come from.'

'Will we see a witch?'

'Certainly,' said Juliet's Grandmamma.

When Juliet woke up she could still feel what she thought was the movement of the ship, only the movement was different, as if the sea wasn't rough any more. She remembered the sea being rough. She remembered the ship going up and then down again, up and down, up and down. She remembered the sound of waves, and people walking unsteadily by where they were sitting, and two girls shrieking because they nearly fell over, and beer from a man's glass spilling on the floor. But Juliet couldn't hear the waves any more, and no one was walking by, unsteadily or otherwise, and everything was quieter.

'We're on the train,' her Grandmamma said.

It was dark outside. It was the middle of the night.

'Gosh!' Juliet said.

'Places have interesting names in Wales,' her Grandmamma said. 'Pontypridd and Abergavenny and Defynnog. Evans and Jones and Thomas are the names of people.'

'Are they nice people?'

'Oh, indeed they are,' her Grandmamma replied in a singsong voice which she said was a Welsh voice. 'And they have a language of their own like we have in Ireland.' She spoke a little of it, and Juliet asked her how she knew it.

'I was in love with a Welshman once,' her Grandmamma said. 'Now, if you listen to me I'll tell you a story about the Witch Who Came for the Weekend. There are a lot of weekend witches in Wales – part-time witches you could call them. Are you hungry?'

'No, not at all.'

'Good. Now listen.'

This time, too, it seemed to Juliet that although the story was about a little Welsh girl called Frances it was also about herself. Frances's friend, the bus driver called Mr Addleripe, was the same kind of friend as Dom's Mr Cranley, and in an odd kind of way reminded Juliet of Paddy Old. The story began with someone called Miss Perego stepping out of a train just like the one Juliet and her

Grandmamma were on.

Miss Perego was wearing a black-and-white striped dress and a wide-brimmed white hat and dark glasses. She waved and smiled at Frances's father. Her teeth were white and there seemed to be a lot of them. She was carrying a small white suitcase and was accompanied by a man called Gareth.

'So this is Frances!' Miss Perego said. She smiled her large white smile and touched Frances's left cheek with the back of her left hand. Her flesh was cold. 'So lovely to meet you, little Frances,' Miss Perego murmured, and the man called Gareth smiled at Frances also.

Frances's father drove the car through the town and out into the country, through the village that was the nearest village to where Frances and her parents lived, and then through the lanes to the farmhouse. All the time Miss Perego talked. She talked about the theatre because Miss Perego was an actress, although not a famous one. Frances had seen her once in a television advertisement for pipe tobacco, in which she looked just like a doll. She had to pretend to be a woman at a garden party who fell in love with a man because he smoked tobacco. Frances's parents had been excited by this, but Frances had considered the whole thing rather silly. In the car on the way to the farmhouse she realised that the man called Gareth was the man in the advertisement.

'My dear, how are you?' Miss Perego cried when Frances's mother came out of the farmhouse with the two collie dogs. 'My dear, how gorgeous!' she cried when the collies barked at her.

It was a pleasant June evening and there was a smell of cows in the yard, and a smell of roses in the kitchen because Frances's mother had picked some specially and put them in two jugs on the dresser. 'My dear, what gorgeous roses!' Miss Perego said, and Frances knew that when they all sat down to supper Miss Perego would say: 'My dear, what gorgeous ham!' which ten minutes later Miss Perego did. The man called Gareth said the ham was gorgeous also.

Frances went to the primary school in the village that was nearest the farmhouse. Every morning she walked half a mile to the crossroads called Moor House Cross, where the school bus picked her up at half-past eight, and every afternoon she walked home from the crossroads. Mr Addleripe, who had been in every country in the world, drove the school bus and knew all about witches. After her mother and her father and her friend, Poppy Jones, Mr Addleripe was the nicest person Frances knew. For the last mile of the journey home with him every afternoon, they were alone together in the bus, and often when he drew the bus up at Moor House Cross they sat a while longer, chatting.

'I knew a witch in China,' Mr Addleripe said. 'Extraordinary girl, no more than sixteen she was.'

The witch in China could control flies, Mr Addleripe said. A Chinese room would be full of flies and the sixteen-year-old witch would enter it and tell them to leave by the window and the flies immediately would. There was another witch he'd come across, a Mrs Llewellyn who owned a chip shop in Swansea, who could control birds. Mrs Llewellyn could stand in a field, still as a statue, and three minutes later birds would be perched all over her. She could walk about the field and the birds would remain with her, some of them apparently asleep.

Mr Addleripe had known Australian and American witches as well as Welsh witches. He'd known African witches who could kill you stone dead just by looking at you, and Egyptian and Norwegian witches and Sicilian witches. He'd known witches in Spain, Denmark, Hungary and France. Twenty-five years ago he'd known one in Greece. Actually, Mr Addleripe said, he'd made a study of witches.

A woman, for instance, might be able to make lemons roll upwards on a slope.

A lot of nonsense was talked about witches, Mr Addleripe said. For a start, no witch ever flew about on a broomstick, nor did witches insist on living in the heart of a forest with only a black cat for company. And all films, stories and television programmes that claimed witches could be here one moment and gone the next were rubbish. There was no such thing as a disappearing witch. If you came across a woman who could disappear like that you were probably in the company of a ghost.

When first he'd talked to her about witches, Frances began to look for them.

'Oh no, no,' he said when she told him that. 'You'll never come across a witch easily, Frances. Your real witch doesn't go around showing off her powers, you know. Your real witch keeps quiet as a mouse about her powers. Naturally enough, Frances: time was, when you caught your witch you burned her.'

Nowadays, Mr Addleripe explained, a lot of witches didn't want to be witches. A woman, for instance, might be able to make lemons roll upwards on a slope, but she'd keep it to herself because men were frightened of stuff like that and wouldn't want to marry such a creature. A woman might be able to control ants, or bees, or hold conversations with horses, but the current

53

fashion was not to admit it. He'd known a woman who used to walk about in a cageful of tigers and another who could bring dead trees to life by touching them. They'd both been in love, the first with a circus clown and the second with a manager of an insurance company, but neither the clown nor the manager had wanted to marry them after they'd heard about the tigers and the trees.

You knew if a woman had witch's powers, Mr Addleripe said, by the nervous way she stood and the nervous way she moved, and by the feel of her flesh. He explained in detail what he meant by the nervous way a witch stood and walked, and in the end Frances understood him. She used to get out of the bus at Moor House Cross and walk through the lanes to the farmhouse, remembering what he'd said and thinking about it. She felt very curious about Mrs Llewellyn who would stand in a field and three minutes later would be covered with birds, and about any woman who could hold conversations with horses, or control flies. She hoped she'd develop a witch's powers herself, but Mr Addleripe said she definitely wouldn't. He could tell just by looking at her, he said.

'Really gorgeous!' Miss Perego said when she'd finished her ham and salad. 'Oh, isn't it nice to be in the country!'

Frances considered that Miss Perego was probably the silliest person she'd ever listened to. Miss Perego had a way of flapping her long, thin hands in the air, and all during supper she kept her white hat on, and her sunglasses. She wasn't at all like Frances's mother, who was pink-cheeked and bustling, or like Frances's father, who didn't say much unless he had a joke to tell. The man called Gareth kept agreeing with everything Miss Perego said in a way that was silly also.

'My dear,' Miss Perego said, 'how gorgeous!'

'Gorgeous!' the man called Gareth said.

They were referring to a dish of strawberries that Frances's mother had placed on the table, and to the jug of yellow cream that went with them. How tedious the weekend was going to be, Frances thought, with Miss Perego saying everything was gorgeous all the time and the man called Gareth agreeing! She wondered where on earth her parents had come across Miss Perego, and seemed to remember her mother saying that they had known her for many years, long before she'd become an actress who wasn't quite famous.

Frances went to bed after the strawberries and cream. She lay awake for ten minutes, gloomily thinking about the boring weekend, with her mother occupied listening to Miss Perego's silly chatter, and her father making hay, and the man called Gareth probably asleep somewhere. She knew that Mr Addleripe would have said Miss Perego had a witch's powers because of the nervous way she'd stepped out of the train and because of her cold flesh, but if this was a witch then a witch wasn't much to write home about. Mr Addleripe might have said that Miss Perego was probably keeping her witch's powers to herself because she wanted the man called Gareth to marry her, but what on earth good was a witch who kept her powers to herself?

Frances, having met at last a woman she could tell Mr Addleripe about, felt most disappointed. She began to think that maybe Mr Addleripe had been having her on, that witches weren't a quarter as interesting as he'd made them out to be. 'Really!' Frances contemptuously exclaimed before she went to sleep. 'Really!'

The next morning Miss Perego sat at the kitchen table while Frances's mother made apple crumble, scones, two sponge cakes and a fruitcake. Frances sat in a corner of the kitchen watching Miss Perego and listening to Miss Perego's silly conversation. The more she watched and listened the more she was convinced that Miss Perego had a witch's powers. She had all the nervousness that Mr Addleripe had described, a nervousness that for all Frances knew could be the cause of her cold flesh.

'Why don't you go out and play, Frances?' Frances's mother said, beating up eggs.

Frances shook her head. Miss Perego laughed.

'Well, you can't sit there all morning, staring at poor Miss Perego. Why don't you go and watch them baling the hay?'

Frances shook her head again.

'Gareth's gone for a walk,' Miss Perego said. 'Why don't you go and look for him?'

'It's rude to stare, dear,' Frances's mother said.

Miss Perego wasn't wearing her white hat, but she'd arrived down to breakfast with her sunglasses on and hadn't taken them off. She'd been sitting at the table for hours, talking about the theatre. Usually on Saturday mornings Frances sat at the table herself, watching her mother and sometimes helping to mix the butter and sugar. She'd often told her mother what Mr Addleripe said in the bus, about witches and the countries he'd visited and the habits that foreign people had, and about when he'd been a child.

'Why don't you ask Poppy over to play this afternoon?' her mother said.

Frances shook her head. She didn't want to ask Poppy Jones over, she said, because she and

Poppy Jones weren't on speaking terms just at the moment.

Miss Perego laughed. 'Let's go and look for Gareth,' she said, and since her mother was glaring at her, Frances decided she'd better go.

They walked through the yard and across the paddock where Frances's father was rearing five heifers. 'We sometimes have lambs here,' Frances told Miss Perego, knowing she had to be polite to the woman.

'How gorgeous!' Miss Perego said.

Frances led the way into the spinney, presuming that the man called Gareth had gone there since it was the walk that people who came for the week-end usually went on. You skirted the big meadow and then clambered down the valley to the river. Miss Perego, Frances saw, would have difficulty because she was wearing unsuitable shoes. Typical, Frances thought.

'There's a man who drives the school bus,' Frances said, 'who knew a Chinese girl who could control flies.'

'Eh?'

'If there were flies in a room this girl could make them go out of the window. Another woman, a Mrs Llewellyn, could control birds. Mrs Llewellyn keeps a chip shop in Swansea.'

'Good heavens!'

'They're women with a witch's powers. Another woman Mr Addleripe knew had conversations with horses.'

Miss Perego, removing a length of bramble from her skirt, did not say anything.

'Another woman could bring dead trees to life by touching them.'

'And can you do anything like that, Frances?'

'No. Can you, Miss Perego?'

Miss Perego laughed.

'It's all nonsense,' Frances said, 'witches having broomsticks and living in a forest. Witches are just like you and me, Miss Perego. Mr Addleripe's made a study of them. Mr Addleripe,' Frances said, following Miss Perego over a stile, 'taught me how to spot a witch at a glance.'

'Good Lord!'

'It's easy, actually.'

Again Miss Perego did not say anything. Frances walked beside her.

'You can tell by the way they move,' Frances said, 'and by the way they stand. And by the coldness of their flesh.'

'I see,' said Miss Perego.

'They're very nervous women, actually.'

They crossed the river on stepping stones and

climbed up through the trees on the other side. They emerged into a sunny field.

'Let's sit down,' Miss Perego said.

They sat on the grass, among daisies and butter-cups.

'What a funny man Mr Addleripe sounds!' Miss Perego said.

'He's one of my best friends.'

'Look,' Miss Perego said.

She pointed at a grass snake that was wriggling its way towards Frances's right leg. Frances gasped. She didn't like snakes. She began to get to her feet but Miss Perego told her not to.

'Sit there,' Miss Perego said in a sharp voice. 'Sit there, Frances, and close your eyes.'

The last thing Frances wanted to do was to close her eyes. If she closed her eyes she'd feel the grass snake crawling on her leg, and she shuddered even at the thought of it.

'Close your eyes,' Miss Perego said again. All the silliness had gone out of her voice. 'Close them.'

Frances did so, and a second could hardly have passed before she heard Miss Perego telling her to open them again. 'Quickly now,' Miss Perego said in the same no-nonsense voice.

The grass snake was no longer there. It couldn't have crawled away in the time. There hadn't even been time for Miss Perego to have picked it up and thrown it into the trees.

'Where is it, Miss Perego?'

'Gone.'

Frances began to get up again, but again Miss Perego told her not to.

'Look,' Miss Perego said.

A ladybird was crawling on to Frances's right leg.

'I quite like ladybirds,' Miss Perego said. 'Don't you, Frances?'

'Yes.'

'I'm so glad,' Miss Perego said softly.

When Miss Perego said that, Frances began to feel frightened of her. She wished she hadn't stared at her in the kitchen. She wished she hadn't begun to talk about witches. It was one thing talking about witches in Mr Addleripe's bus; it was quite another to be sitting in a field with a witch who'd just turned a grass snake into a ladybird. Miss Perego seemed all the more frightening because she'd been so silly and now was so serious. Miss Perego wasn't laughing, she wasn't even smiling. Not in a hundred years would you have guessed that Miss Perego had once been like a doll in a television advertisement for tobacco.

'Sounds a bit of a silly,' Miss Perego said as softly

as before, 'that Mr Addleripe.'

'Oh, no . . .'

'Silly to talk about witches like that, I'd have said. Silly to be too interested, you know.'

The ladybird crawled along Frances's leg. Did it know it was a ladybird? Frances wondered. Did it still imagine it was a grass snake? Would she know she was Frances if she changed into something else? Would she feel like Frances even though she'd suddenly become a horsefly?

'Ladybirds are harmless,' Miss Perego said quietly.

They walked from the field together, down into the valley and across the stepping stones in the river and up the other side, skirting the meadow, through the paddock and the yard. At lunch Miss Perego was her old silly self again, and as Frances listened to her chatter and her laughter she seemed more frightening even than she'd seemed before.

For the rest of that weekend Miss Perego giggled and said things were gorgeous. She said it was gorgeous that Frances's father had finished haymaking, and that the sponge cakes and the scones and the fruit-cake were gorgeous. She sat at the kitchen table, chattering to Frances's mother. She said what fun it had been making the television advertisement for pipe tobacco.

'Ladybirds are harmless,' Miss Perego said quietly.

'Goodbye, Frances,' Miss Perego said on Sunday evening. She held out her right hand and Frances felt the cold flesh, and for a moment could hardly believe that any person could be so silly and also be so frightening. Miss Perego smiled at her.

'I hope the weekend wasn't too boring for you, Frances,' Miss Perego said.

'Oh no, Miss Perego.'

'Do give my love to that Mr Addleripe of yours.'

The next afternoon, when she sat alone with Mr Addleripe in his bus, Frances wanted to tell him about Miss Perego and to ask him what he thought. She wanted to describe Miss Perego, her crowded mouthful of teeth and her dark glasses and her pretend silliness and her white hat. She wanted to mention the man called Gareth whom Miss Perego hoped to marry, who'd appeared in the tobacco advertisement with her. But she didn't. 'A nice lady came for the weekend,' she said instead.

Chapter 4

Juliet and her grandmamma had breakfast on the train, which by now had passed through Wales and was in England. When they reached London a tall, very thin man waved at them from the platform.

He shook hands with Juliet and with her Grandmamma and said he was delighted to see them. Juliet considered him by far the most polite person she had ever encountered. He had a blue scarf with little white dots, and a tie that matched it, and a watch-chain running across his waistcoat, from one pocket to another. He carried their suitcases, just as the man with the moustache had in Dublin. He opened the door of a taxi for them and put the suitcases in the front, beside the driver. Juliet's Grandmamma said she could sleep for a week.

'Have a doze, old girl,' the polite man urged, and then he pointed out the sights to Juliet, who wouldn't have had a doze for anything.

No one was about because it was so early in the morning. A few cats sat on doorsteps or sniffed at the bags of garbage that hadn't been collected yet. Sometimes a poor old tramp hunched his way along the pavement, rooting in the litter-bins in the hope of finding something to eat. People who worked at night were going home, but there weren't very many of them.

'Look!' the polite man said, and Juliet saw that the window of a shop had been smashed in the night. 'Robbers,' the polite man said.

Policemen stood around, one of them talking into a radio, another measuring the window, the others just watching.

'Look!' the polite man said a moment later, and Juliet saw a very tall stone pillar with a figure on top of it, and four stone lions crouching in protection. 'That's one-eyed Nelson,' the man said. 'Admiral Lord Nelson,' he added more solemnly.

The taxi drew up at another railway station. 'Called after a certain Queen Victoria,' the polite man said. 'As many a place in England is.'

Juliet's Grandmamma woke up. She scolded the polite man for letting her fall asleep, but he was busy lifting the suitcases out of the taxi and paying the driver.

'There we are,' he said soothingly, settling Juliet and her Grandmamma into another railway carriage. He went away and returned with newspapers and magazines, and hot coffee and apples and bananas. Then he said he'd better be off or else he'd be carried away with them.

'What a very long journey it is!' Juliet said, peeling an apple with a very tiny penknife her Grandmamma carried in her handbag. It was the prettiest penknife Juliet had ever seen. Her Grandmamma said it had a mother-of-pearl handle.

'You're never *bored*?' she asked, alarmed when Juliet remarked that it was a long journey.

Juliet shook her head emphatically.

'That's all right then.'

The train passed through the hop-fields of Kent. In the far distance a great house stood on a hill, its gardens spread all about it. A long drive with trees on either side of it led up to the hall door.

'Shall I tell you my English story?', Juliet's Grandmamma asked, 'since we are passing through England?'

'Yes, please.'

Again it seemed to Juliet that although the story took place far back in time, the girl in it was really herself. And as if guessing what was in her mind, her Grandmamma said:

'When we come to the old grandmother you mustn't think of me because this one is all wizened and bent. Twice as old as I am, I'd say. I'd like you to remember that.'

'Yes, of course,' Juliet politely agreed.

'The Gate-girl and the Snail', her Grandmamma said.

Once upon a time, a very long time ago, Annabella lived in a small house beside the gates at the end of a drive. The drive, which became very dark in summer because the leaves of the trees kept out the sunlight, led to a house that was a very great deal larger than the house beside the gates. It had ninety-one rooms and the smaller house had only three. It had halls and passages, and landings on the first floor and landings on the second, and back sculleries, and pantries and larders, and a fountain and statues in the garden. Nettlehampton Court it was called. The house where Annabella lived with her grandmother and grandfather wasn't called anything at all.

Before the time Annabella could remember, her father had gone away, to walk to a town where he had heard there was work. When he did not return her mother went to look for him.

'What happened was that both of them must have met up with the King's soldiers and the Roundheads,' Annabella's grandmother said when Annabella asked her, for at the time there had been fighting between two different armies. That was how Annabella came to be in the house by the gates, where her mother had left her in the care of her grandmother and her grandfather. She couldn't remember being anywhere else.

The gates were tall and white, with a row of spikes at the top. They were heavy because they were made of iron, but they were easy to open and close because Annabella's grandfather kept them oiled. 'See to the gates, Annabella,' her grandmother would say.

'There's someone waiting there.' The gates were always kept closed in case the cows wandered up the drive and ate the flowers in the garden. When her grandmother said to see to them, Annabella would run out and pull up the shaft that held the gates steady. She would lift the huge latch that secured one gate to the other, and then she would push them open and stand at the side while a horse and cart or a carriage passed through. The driver always called out to her, thanking her, sometimes waving his whip. Then she would carefully close the gates again, and sometimes when she looked down the road she could see the cows grazing on the verges, pretending not to notice her, but she knew they were keen to come in. The grass in the garden would taste better, her grandfather said – there wasn't grass to touch it for miles around. Her grandfather knew what he was talking about, being one of the gardeners at Nettlehampton Court. People called Annabella the gate-girl.

One night when she couldn't go to sleep Annabella heard her grandparents talking in the kitchen and when she heard her own name mentioned she naturally listened.

'I'm wondering,' her grandfather said, 'what will become of her.'

'Isn't she warm and dry?' her grandmother replied tartly. 'Hasn't she shoes on her feet? Hasn't she food when she's hungry?'

'She's stuck here with ourselves though.'

'What's wrong with that?'

'Two old ones is what I'm saying. What companions are we?'

'Better than none.'

'It's not much fun, opening and closing the gates, day in, day out.'

'Fun? What's she want fun for?'

'It's just that I thought –'

'Drink up your tea.'

Annabella fell asleep, but the next day she had to open and close the gates more times than usual and while she was doing it she kept thinking about what had been said. The first person she opened them for was a man on a cart who had chickens to sell to the cook at Nettlehampton Court.

'Are you keeping well, Annabella?' he enquired as he went by, for he always had a word for her.

She said she was well and asked how he was himself. All right except for a soreness in his back due to lifting a heavy rock, he said.

The next people who appeared were two gipsy women who wanted to go up to Nettlehampton Court with clothes-pegs to sell. When they lifted the latch of the gates Annabella's grandmother heard the sound and told her to hurry out and shoo them away.

'There's not better pegs the length and breadth of England,' one of the women protested when Annabella shoo-ed them. 'If five gales were blow-ing, the wind wouldn't shift a stitch off the line when the washing was held by these pegs.'

But Annabella held on to the gates and wouldn't let the gipsy women open them any further. She had to do as she was told, she said.

The next people to arrive were some of the

family from Nettlehampton Court, going the other way. They were in the green jaunting-carriage, the boy and the girl and their beautiful older sister. The boy and the girl were about the same age as Annabella. The girl had dark ringlets and a little blue coat with a trimming of fur on it. The boy was in a brown velvet suit. They didn't say anything when Annabella opened the gates for them, nor did their beautiful sister. But Cyril, who was driving the jaunting-car, winked at her.

Then the grocery cart arrived, and after that the fish cart. 'I was remarking to them in the kitchen,' the man who'd sold the chickens to the cook called out to her on his way out through the gates again, 'I was remarking that it's maybe the first day of summer. Would you agree with that, Annabella?'

She said she would because it was easier to agree than not to, and when the grocery man and the fish man were passing through the gates again, they, too, made a reference to the weather. Both of them laughed when she said it was maybe the first day of summer.

Annabella guessed that the boy and girl from Nettlehampton Court had gone shopping with their sister. She guessed that later on they would return with the jaunting-car full of parcels, and that they'd be talking excitedly. If it wasn't that particular boy and girl who went shopping it was other members of the family, even Mr and Mrs Nettlehampton themselves. Altogether there were nine in the family, seven of them children of different ages.

'Keep a good watch out for those gipsies,' her grandmother had instructed. 'They'll be down round the bend in the road waiting for a chance to slip in. Worse than the cows they are.'

So Annabella sat on the road with her back against one of the gate pillars, keeping a look out. All the time she was thinking about what had been said the night before. She had often wondered what it was like to be one of the children who passed through the gates. Sometimes, on a very quiet day, she heard their voices carrying through the trees from the garden and knew that they were playing a game. She often wondered what it was like to have companions.

Later that same day, after the gipsy women had made four more attempts to come in the gates, the boy and girl and their sister returned. Cyril winked at Annabella again and the parcels were there, just as Annabella had imagined. Afterwards Annabella heard voices and laughter coming from the garden. Once a kite appeared above the trees, a red-and-blue kite with ribbons trailing behind it.

'Well, did you take care of the gates for your grandmother?' her grandfather asked when he returned from his work in the garden.

She said she'd done so. She told him about the fish cart and grocery cart and the man with the chickens, and the gipsies.

'Where'd we be without Annabella?' her grandfather asked her grandmother, but all her grandmother replied was that they would probably be where they were before Annabella had been left with them.

'We'd be lost without Annabella,' her grandfather insisted firmly.

Annabella knew he was only saying it. It was a nuisance for them that her mother hadn't come back for her. She wouldn't be occupying the extra room if her mother had come back. In the past it used to be a little parlour, where her grandparents might sit on a Sunday, and all the ornaments and pictures were still there. There was a seashell you could hear the sea in when you put it up to your ear, and a cup with roses on it, and a framed picture of a man with a beard, and china figures in a glass-fronted cupboard, as well as chairs and a table.

'Eat up your tea, Annabella,' her grandmother said sharply. 'Don't be gawping.'

'I was only thinking.'

Annabella did not go to school. Her grandmother taught her the letters of the alphabet when she had time, and after he'd had his tea her grandfather taught her to count. She had a slate that he'd brought back from Nettlehampton Court when it fell off the roof in a storm. She made the letters of the alphabet on it with pieces of chalk, and all the numbers from nought to nine. It was the best that could be done, her grandparents said.

That evening, after her grandfather had had his tea, Annabella wrote the numbers she knew on the slate and showed him each one when it was ready. All the time she was doing it she kept imagining the children playing in the garden with a new coloured ball they'd bought, and then flying a different kite. She imagined them hiding from one another and running races, and all of them sitting down to their tea together. They talked about the shopping they'd done and the different people they'd met in the town.

Days went by, all of them like that. Annabella opened and closed the gates for the fish cart and the grocery cart and for Cyril, and for other people who came and went. She practised her letters and her numbers and she thought about the children playing in the garden. She thought about them more and more, wondering what it was like to play, because she had never played with anyone. She wondered if she would ever see the house at the end of the drive. 'What you might call a palace,' her grandfather said when she asked him.

One night, after her grandmother and grandfather had gone to bed, the moon was like daylight in her room, showing up all the ornaments and the framed picture of the man with the beard. The moon would be shining in the garden too, on the flowers and the flowerbeds, just as though it were daytime. It would be shining all over the house that was like a palace.

Annabella rose and dressed herself. She opened her door very softly, and listened. She could hear breathing coming from the other bedroom and knew by the sound of it that her grandparents were asleep. She crept through the kitchen and pulled back the bolts of the door.

She made her way through a shrubbery, passing in and out of pools of darkness because the moon was often obscured by high trees. An owl kept hooting. A rabbit scampered across her path.

When she emerged she found herself on a huge lawn of closely cut grass. Ahead of her were five circular rosebeds and beyond them the house was just as she'd imagined. A great array of windows gleamed in the moonlight. A wide flight of steps led up to pillars and a white hall door.

She could have looked at it forever, Annabella thought. She could have stood on the edge of the grass, staring over the circular rosebeds at the gravel sweep in front of the house, at the rows of windows, at the pillars and the white hall door. The roses were all different shades of red, but on either side of the lawn there were long borders full of blue flowers and yellow flowers, and flowers that were purple and pink and orange and silvery. Annabella didn't know the names of any of them.

While she was standing there she saw something moving. There was a tree with spreading branches on one side of the house, its leaves making a ragged shadow on the grass. Out of this shadow something was slowly making its way – an enormous snail it seemed to be.

Annabella watched. The snail advanced in a waggling, stuttering motion, its whole body wrenched from side to side each time it took a step. Then, to Annabella's astonishment, it began to get smaller. And it didn't stutter and waggle but crept slowly along, dragging itself over the ground. It was grey, with swirls of brown in the shell it carried on its back. Its movement had become extremely slow and it was now no bigger than a snail usually is. The moonlight had been playing

*Something was slowly making its way – an enormous snail
it seemed to be.*

tricks, she said to herself. Moonshine was tricky stuff, her grandfather used occasionally to remark; you couldn't trust it an inch.

'He's right enough,' someone said to her, making her jump. 'Your grandfather didn't come down in the last shower of rain.'

She turned quickly around. She peered into the shrubbery behind her. She couldn't see anyone.

'It's me,' the same voice said, and she could have sworn it was Cyril talking to her because of the way certain words were pronounced.

'You'd have been right if you *had* sworn it,' the voice said. 'You'd have been right if you'd placed a bet on it. You could have won a fortune. I borrowed the voice from Cyril because Cyril's asleep. What use is a voice to a man who's asleep?'

'No use,' Annabella said, feeling she should say something but also feeling just a little frightened.

'No need to be frightened when it's only a poor old snail who's involved in this. I don't know if you noticed, but there's a snail approaching you.'

Suddenly Annabella wanted to go back to her grandparents' house. She wanted to hurry through the trees of the shrubbery and then round the last bit of the avenue and creep in through the door she'd left open. She wanted to pull the bedclothes up over her head. But when she tried to move,

Cyril's voice said:

'You should have thought of that before you decided it was a good idea to go wandering into the night. Moonlight or not.'

'I wanted to see the house. And the garden as well.'

'You have an inquisitive nature, Annabella.'

'I suppose I have.'

'People with inquisitive natures end up disastrously. Another way of saying that is to remark that they bite off more than they can chew. Didn't your grandfather ever tell you that?'

'No, he didn't.'

'I would call that negligence.'

'I think I'd better be getting back.'

'That's not true. What you think is: It's peculiar to be conducting a conversation with a snail.'

'Snails can't talk.'

'You put that badly. "As a general rule of nature," you should have said, "snails can't talk."'

'I'm sorry.'

'I have explained to you what has happened. In a perfectly reasonable manner the voice of the man who drives the jaunting-car has been borrowed. It's not the best voice in the world, I'd be the first to say that. It's not the prettiest, nor the clearest. There's a difficulty with the "h". 'Ouse, 'im, 'it, 'urry. That's the way the jaunting-car man talks. On an occasion like this I find it embarrassing.'

She was still in her bed, Annabella thought. She was asleep and dreaming. She'd been fast asleep and she'd dreamed about the moonlight, and about getting up and creeping through the kitchen, about the shrubbery and the garden and the house and all of it. But especially about a snail who had begun by being five times the size it was now.

'You're deliberately misleading yourself,' came the contradiction, promptly. 'You're neither in your bed nor are you dreaming, nor both. You are having a conversation with a member of the animal kingdom. It's a one-sided conversation because you are affected by wonder and bewilderment.'

'It feels like dreaming.'

'On some other occasion we might discuss that at length. For the time being, take my word for it that dreams do not come into this. Neither you nor I have entered dreamland.'

'Well . . .'

'The people in that house are dreaming, the jaunting-car man among them. Mr Nettlehampton is dreaming he's riding a horse in a desert, and Mrs Nettlehampton that she is washing a lettuce. Other dreams – those of children and servants – have to do with bluebirds, and toppling off towers, and giving sermons in churches, and being put in a coffin by mistake. As well, there are dreams concerning rosemary picked from a vegetable patch, and a jampot floating on the sea, and dreams of being chased by wolves, tigers, giraffes and German bears. A snail can chase nothing or no one, as you probably know.'

'I still think –'

'Doesn't your grandmother teach you manners?'

'Yes, she does.'

'Well, she doesn't make much of a job of it, does she? You are exceedingly rude, you know. No sooner is something remarked upon than you contradict it.'

'I'm very sorry.'

Annabella turned to go away, but the snail called after her.

'Come back another night,' he begged, changing his tune considerably.

'Why should I?'

'Because it's lonely,' the snail said meekly. 'All night long it's lonely in this garden. No one in the big house comes into it at night-time because they're daytime people. Only little girls who are all on their own are equipped to have conversations with lonely snails.'

'Honestly?'

'A snail cannot tell a lie any more than it can perform in a circus.'

And every night after that Annabella slipped out of bed and went to meet her friend, and every day she thought about what they said to one another. She heard the children's voices in the garden and opened the gates for them when they went shopping. But she knew that no matter how many different games they played, or how much fun they had, or how many toys they possessed, there was nothing in their lives as marvellous as being able to have conversations with a snail that could borrow people's voices and tell you people's dreams.

When the story came to an end Juliet was glad she was really herself and not a girl who had been left in a gate-house, opening and shutting gates all day – even if it did mean that to make up for it she could converse with snails. She was glad she had Kitty Ann. The first thing she'd do when they arrived at wherever they were going would be to send Kitty Ann a picture postcard.

CHAPTER 5

The train continued to rattle on, and then there was another crossing on a boat, and then another train, which was different because it was French. The sun came out during the last bit of the journey. 'Oh, lovely!' Juliet's Grandmamma said.

They were in a little seaside place when the train stopped, and everyone had to get off because it didn't go any further. Looking out from the car that drove them to the hotel where they were going to stay, Juliet noticed that all the rocks that the sea washed over were white, and that the lighthouse that was built on the biggest rock of all was white also. Yachts and sailing-boats and motor-boats were tied up in the harbour. There were jolly-looking cafés and restaurants along the sea-front, and fish for sale on stalls. The air smelt salty.

'What d'you think of it?' Juliet's Grandmamma asked.

'It's lovely.'

'I think so. I love it here.'

The hotel was called Le Roc Blanc, which Juliet's Grandmamma said meant the white rock. The car drove through white gates, which reminded Juliet of the gates in the story about the gate-girl and the snail because they were big and high. They had the look of gates that are never closed, as if they were kept there just for decoration.

The hotel was white also and had a terrace running along the front of it, with tables and chairs. You had to pass through it in order to reach the front door, which was wide open also. A few people were reading at the tables. At one table two men were playing cards, with a dog asleep by their feet.

'We're expected, I hope?' Juliet's Grandmamma said in the hall. The girl behind the desk said yes, they were.

'Pierre!' she called out, and a man in shirtsleeves with a green baize apron came to take their suitcases and show them to their rooms.

When Juliet and her Grandmamma had unpacked, they went for a walk in the hotel gardens and then they climbed down to a little bay and had a swim in the sea.

'You'll be hungry?' Juliet's Grandmamma said as they walked back to the hotel with their wet towels and bathing-suits.

'Well, a little.'

'The sea makes you hungry.'

Juliet would have liked to stay longer in the little bay. In the pools among the rocks she'd seen shrimps, and there were brown rubbery blobs clinging to the rocks that her Grandmamma said were a kind of fish. Shells clung to the rocks also and there were tiny jellyfish, like stars.

'I wonder how everything is at home.'

Her Grandmamma laughed. 'It's a long way to Tipperary,' she said.

'I hope they're all right.'

'Put them out of your mind. When you're on holiday you must always put things out of your mind.'

But Juliet found it hard to do that. She kept thinking of hiding under Lawlor's Bridge and in the old graveyard, and of walking by the high stone warehouses on the river, and of lying on the grass in Dandelion Meadow. She saw P.J. Kelly's hotel clearly and the brass plates of the doctors and solicitors, and the men standing round in the shop that didn't sell anything, excited because horses were racing on television. The Galtee Mountains pressed down on the town, and the streets and the square were grey and sunless.

That evening Juliet sent picture postcards to her mother and father. She sent one to Kitty Ann, telling her about everything, as though they were friends as usual. She remembered fat Declan Flynn saying you had to die when you were that age, and she realised what she hadn't realised before: that he had been trying to be sympathetic. She sent him a postcard too, with a picture of the lighthouse on it. She sent one to Sister Catherine and one to Miss Walsh. She would have sent one to the Russian Princess except that she didn't know how to address it.

'*Bon soir, madame!*' the waiter said in the dining-room. '*Bon soir, mademoiselle!*' he said to Juliet.

Juliet's Grandmamma was wearing a red-and-white dress, in stripes, and a man with a beard smiled at her as she passed, but she didn't notice so Juliet smiled back instead. Table 12 was their table. The man with the beard was on his own, two tables away.

'I think that man knows you, Grandmamma,' Juliet whispered, for the man had raised his glass in the air and was bowing and smiling in their direction.

'Certainly not,' her Grandmamma said. 'Take no notice.'

The waiter brought their soup and a little basket of bread. The bread was fresh and crusty. The soup was delicious.

'*Pardon, madame,*' the man with the beard said, pausing by their table on his way out of the dining-room. He had a nice pink face, Juliet considered – at least the part of it that wasn't hidden by his beard was pink – and pleasant eyes, as blue as Kitty Ann's.

'Yes?' Juliet's Grandmamma sounded quite rude and snappish. 'Yes?' she repeated in the same abrupt way.

'Welcome, *madame.*'

'What do you want?'

'We have met before, *madame.* I am sure of it.'

'Certainly not.'

'In this hotel, *madame*? Three summers ago?' Quite unperturbed by the reception he was receiving, the man held out a hand. 'Marcel Vapp. At your service, *madame*!'

'Monsieur Vapp!'

'The beard disguises Monsieur Vapp! Welcome back to Le Roc Blanc.'

Monsieur Vapp pressed a thumb and forefinger together,
touched them with his lips and then made a gesture
in the air.

Juliet noticed that her Grandmamma had turned almost as pink as Monsieur Vapp. Her mouth had fallen open with surprise. She closed it hastily and shook Monsieur Vapp's hand.

'This is my – well, my granddaughter,' she said, a little reluctantly, Juliet thought.

'*Mon Dieu!*' cried Monsieur Vapp. 'How could you possibly be old enough for a granddaughter?'

'I don't feel it.'

'You don't look it, my dear. It's an absurdity!'

'I'm from County Tipperary,' Juliet said, feeling she should say something, since both her grandmother and Monsieur Vapp were now looking at her as though she could not possibly exist.

'*Nom d'un nom!* It's a long way to Tipperary, eh? And you are called, *ma petite*? You have a pretty little name?'

'Juliet.'

'Juliet!' Monsieur Vapp pressed a thumb and forefinger together, touched them with his lips and then made a gesture in the air. Juliet was his very favourite name, he said. 'Assuredly!' he exclaimed. 'Most certainly and assuredly a beautiful name!'

'I'm sorry I didn't recognise you,' Juliet's Grandmamma apologised.

'Then make up for the lapse by taking a cognac with me later!'

'That is most kind of you, Monsieur Vapp.'

Monsieur Vapp bowed and passed on.

'What a nice man!' Juliet whispered.

'Oh, he's all right.'

But Juliet could tell that her Grandmamma considered Monsieur Vapp rather more than all right and wondered if she was in love with him, as she had been with the Welshman she'd spoken of, and as Miss Perego had been with Gareth.

'I wish I had a story of my own,' Juliet said while they were waiting for the waiter to come and take away their soup plates.

'What d'you mean, Juliet?'

'Like that Annabella had. And Dom. And Frances. And Conal and Donal and Taig. And the Man Who Lost His Shadow, and the Man Who Swallowed the Mouse, and –'

'Oh, don't worry. You'll have stories enough before you've finished.'

'Will I really?'

'Most certainly and assuredly,' Juliet's Grandmamma promised, and they both laughed.

'We have the trouts,' the waiter said. 'A speciality of Le Roc Blanc. Look, I show.'

In a very expert way he slipped away their soup plates and then wheeled a trolley across the dining-room to their table. On it there was a glass tank full of water. Fish were swimming in it.

'*Voilà!*' the waiter announced proudly.

Juliet didn't understand. She didn't know why they were being shown live fish when they were naturally expecting a plate of something.

'D'you like trout, Juliet?' her Grandmamma asked.

Juliet frowned, still not understanding.

'You pick one out and they'll cook it for you,' her Grandmamma explained.

'But they're swimming about! They're still alive!'

'Fresh,' the waiter put in. 'You get them fresh.'

'It's horrid,' Juliet said, and looked away in case she met the eye of one of the unfortunate trout.

'We'll have the chicken *à la king*,' her Grandmamma hastily decided, and the trolley was wheeled away.

'Really horrid!' Juliet cried. 'Poor little things!'

'I'm afraid it's the way of the world,' her Grandmamma said.

'It's not the way of *my* world.' Juliet made her voice as indignant as she could manage. It was all very well for her Grandmamma, looking forward to her cognac with Monsieur Vapp. It was all very well for the waiter, who had wheeled the trolley to another table. A woman in a purple dress was pointing at one of the trout, and a sad-looking man who was with her pointed at another. Juliet could see a very thin couple peering at fish bones on their plates, winkling pieces of flesh from them. A second waiter was placing two trout in front of the men who had been playing cards on the terrace. A fat woman was asking for more.

'Don't have a tantrum, dear.' Juliet's grandmother employed her no-nonsense voice. 'Nobody has a tantrum on a holiday.'

Juliet said she was sorry even though she didn't feel it. Really! she thought, and when eventually they left the dining-room they had to pass quite close to the fish tank. She actually caught the eye of the smallest trout, although she didn't want to.

'Poor little pet,' she kept saying to herself before she went to sleep that night. '*Poor* little pet!'

Juliet dreamed she was back in the town. The Angelus bell was ringing and when it stopped Kitty Ann said, 'Come down to the sawmills.' On the way they looked in the shop windows – at the winter overcoats in Phelan's, and the fruit and boxes of chocolates in Fennerty's, and cut-price soups in Kitty Ann's own shop.

'Hey, look at that!' Kitty Ann exclaimed when they'd gone on a bit, and there was Declan Flynn lying down in the middle of the street with his eyes closed.

'Is Declan dead?' Kitty Ann asked in an awestruck voice, but Juliet said no, only lying there to show he was lazier than Donal or Taig. 'If five lorries and a dozen tractors were coming towards him he wouldn't stir,' she said.

They watched timber being sawn at the sawmills and they climbed up steep Castle Hill to the ruins. The Russian Princess was sitting on a tumbled-down wall. 'If you listen I'll tell you my story,' she said, and she did, only in the language that nobody could understand. Her story was that all her life no one could understand her, and she was crying, saying it was a terrible fate.

'We all have a story,' Paddy Old said, stepping out of the castle ruins.

Then they were in Dandelion Meadow with Madra, who was barking at the crickets. Sister Catherine and Miss Walsh were stitching the same piece of knitting and there was another woman in the meadow and that was the weekend witch. The sunflowers wouldn't come until it snowed, the Welsh witch said, and Sister Catherine and Miss Walsh nodded their heads in agreement. Their knitting was looped between them, getting longer all the time; purple and gold it was, knitted curtains for the pantomime because the old curtains had worn out.

In South Main Street there were pork steaks and chops laid out in a butcher's window ready to be sold, and sausages and legs of lamb and a kidney. All of them were talking to one another. 'It's the kidney's birthday,' said a snail.

Then Juliet woke up, with sunshine warm on her face, and she couldn't think where she was. Slowly she remembered: the little room with only one picture on the cream-coloured wall opposite her bed was in France. The journey came rushing back to her – the teasing man with the drooping moustache, and the polite man, and at the end of the journey, Monsieur Vapp. She could hear the sea, and when she looked out of the window she saw the pale rocks far down below her, and sparkles of sunlight dancing over the blue surface of the water.

CHAPTER 6

Juliet and her grandmother and Monsieur Vapp walked from the hotel to the harbour. They sat at a café called Le Zeff and had coffee.

'Like to wander round, dear?' Juliet's Grand-mamma suggested, noticing that Juliet wasn't much interested in the conversation she was having with Monsieur Vapp. 'Keep in sight and look back and wave every few minutes.'

'No further than the boat with the red sails,' Monsieur Vapp warned. 'We'd be upset if we lost you.'

So Juliet went off on her own, glancing back at the café called Le Zeff every minute or so. She walked on the quayside, watching people scrubbing the decks of their boats or painting bits of them or doing things with ropes. One or two of the people waved at her.

'*C'est magnifique!*' she heard a voice call out loudly, as if keen to attract attention. She turned her head and noticed a small man in a blue-and-white striped T-shirt and a beret, surrounded by a lot of mechanical toys. There were children on some of the boats, and he was doing his best to attract their attention. But only a baby, being wheeled past in a pram, was interested in him. The little man made a huge, brightly-coloured top spin, and as it did so it played a tune. There were little hens among the toys, and ducks that nodded, and a pig and a cow that moved, and a snake that crawled. Juliet went closer, trying to see if there was a bird like the one she'd been given for her birthday, but there wasn't.

'*Bonjour, mademoiselle,*' the little man greeted her, and then said something else in French that Juliet didn't even begin to understand.

She shook her head.

'You come from England?' the little man asked.

'From Ireland. County Tipperary.'

Juliet said that because she wanted to see if he'd say it was a long way to Tipperary, as Monsieur Vapp had. But he didn't.

'Very good toys,' was what he said instead.

Juliet went closer, trying to see if there was a bird like the one she'd been given for her birthday.

'Very cheap.'

'Very nice,' Juliet said.

'You like the pig? The crocodile? The spinning top?'

She shook her head.

'I haven't any money,' she explained.

'Perhaps to get a few francs?' the little man suggested. 'Perhaps some kind father or kind mother?'

While he spoke he held out a toy she hadn't seen before. It wriggled and twisted on the palm of his hand. Juliet began to laugh because for some reason the wriggling was funny.

'*C'est bon?*' the little man said. '*C'est magnifique?*'

It was a fish. It looked just like the smallest trout in the dining-room tank.

'I have better, more expensive.' The little man reached into a large blue box on the quay at his feet and produced two larger fish. 'Three size we have.'

He showed Juliet how to wind up the fish, in just the same way as the bird that flapped its wings was wound up.

'You speak very good English,' she remarked politely. She felt she should, since he was being so pleasant even though she hadn't any money.

'I sell the toys in Scotland once. All one years

I sell. Edinburgh. Aberdeen. Glasgow. You know Scotland?'

'I know where it is.'

'Bagpipes. Bonny Prince Charlie. Mutton pies. Very good country.'

'I'm afraid I must go now.'

'You come back again? Which toy you like?'

'The fish.'

'I keep the fish for you.'

'Well, the thing is . . .'

'Is no trouble.'

Juliet said goodbye and returned to the Le Zeff.

'Interesting walk?' her grandmother enquired.

'Lovely,' Juliet said.

'We've been getting on like a house on fire here,' Monsieur Vapp revealed, and Juliet saw her grandmother going pink again. 'Am I right?' Monsieur Vapp asked. 'A house on fire you say?'

'Yes,' Juliet said.

'Funny thing to get on like,' her grandmother observed, 'I always think.'

On the way back to the hotel Juliet's Grand-mamma went into a shop to buy a spool of thread and Monsieur Vapp and Juliet waited outside. He asked her if she'd seen anything interesting on the quays and she told him about the little man and the toys.

'Toys, eh?'

'The kind you wind up. A cow and a pig. Hens and ducks, and a crocodile and a snake. And trout.'

'Trout?'

'I think they were. They looked like trout. They were fish anyway.'

'And which among these toys did you like best, Juliet?'

'Oh, the trout. Easily.'

That evening in the dining-room Monsieur Vapp shared table 12 with Juliet and her Grandmamma, and when the fish-tank was wheeled up he pointed at the plumpest of the trout and said he'd like it grilled for him. Juliet and her Grandmamma had roast beef.

'The best thing about Le Roc Blanc is the dining-room,' Monsieur Vapp said. 'I've often remarked there isn't a better dining-room in France.'

'By that Monsieur Vapp means the food,' Juliet's Grandmamma explained. 'When you say dining-room in France you usually mean what you eat in it.'

Monsieur Vapp nodded and beamed, his pleasant eyes pleasanter than ever. In the afternoon he'd had a swim with them and he had helped Juliet to collect shells in the rockpools. His swimming trunks were pink, like his face.

'Delicious!' he exclaimed when his fish came. At least it wasn't the smallest one; perhaps no one would ever choose the smallest one, Juliet thought, because it looked so undernourished. Unless of course it put on weight.

'What shall we do tomorrow, eh?' Monsieur Vapp asked. 'Shall I take you for a drive? Or a game of clock golf? Or tennis? Eh, Juliet?'

'Clock golf would be nice.'

Juliet kept her eyes on her own plate so that she wouldn't have to see Monsieur Vapp's knife and fork. Once when she looked up there was a tiny fish-bone caught in his beard. He was as hungry as a hunter, he said, smacking his lips and now and again touching them with an edge of his napkin.

'Fish is good for the brain,' he said between mouthfuls.

'And potatoes are good for the memory,' Juliet's Grandmamma chattily added.

'And carrots for seeing in the dark.'

'And spinach for strength, of course.'

'An apple a day.'

'Oh, you are a one, Monsieur Vapp!'

Juliet didn't contribute to this conversation because she considered it rather silly. At least

'Look!' exclaimed Monsieur Vapp suddenly, pointing
at the sky.

the very thin couple weren't having fish from the trout-tank tonight, nor was the woman in the purple dress. That at least was something. All the time Juliet had been splashing about in the sea she'd thought about the trout in the fish-tank, patiently waiting for someone to eat them. It didn't feel right to be in the sea while they were trapped in a tank. After all, the sea was their home, it wasn't hers. They'd feel free in the sea, with the sand and pebbles, and the rocks to swim around, and the bottoms of the yachts going by.

'And goats' milk for beauty,' Monsieur Vapp was saying. He winked at Juliet's Grandmamma, who told him to get on with himself.

When the fish-tank was wheeled round again Juliet saw that the smallest trout was still there. She counted seven others. Poor little pets! she thought again.

The next day Juliet played clock golf with her Grandmamma and Monsieur Vapp. First Monsieur Vapp won, then her Grandmamma did, and then Juliet did. After that they sat at Café Le Zeff and watched the people going by. They drank apricot juice, which was delicious.

'Look!' exclaimed Monsieur Vapp suddenly, pointing at the sky.

A huge balloon was slowly rising, floating up and up above the harbour. Attached to it was a basket, in which there were people, one of them holding what seemed to be a dog.

'Gosh!' Juliet cried, opening her eyes very wide the way her father said she always did when something spectacular occurred.

The balloon was yellow and blue and red, and now and again an orange flame spurted out of some kind of container between the balloon itself and the basket. Whenever the flame came there was a loud rushing noise.

'Gas,' Monsieur Vapp explained knowledgeably.

'What does the gas do?' Juliet's Grandmamma asked.

'Hot air rises,' Monsieur Vapp replied, a little more vaguely. 'Look!' he exclaimed again, and Juliet guessed he didn't want to explain *exactly* about the hot air and the gas.

'Look, they're waving!' Monsieur Vapp said, and waved back.

Juliet waved too, but her Grandmamma just smiled.

'I wonder.' Monsieur Vapp stroked his beard, which was a habit of his when he was thinking. 'I wonder,' he said again.

The balloon was floating away quite quickly

now. You could hardly see the people in the basket and certainly not the dog. Monsieur Vapp suddenly stood up and strode off into the café. Juliet could hear him talking excitedly in French.

'Exactly so,' he said when he returned to their table. 'We can go for a joy ride in it ourselves.'

'Not me,' Juliet's Grandmamma said firmly. 'Not on your life.'

'Eh, Juliet?'

'Yes, *please*.'

So Juliet's Grandmamma returned to the hotel and Juliet and Monsieur Vapp took a taxi through the town to where the balloon station was. This was a large field, and by the time they reached it the balloon was coming in to land.

'Gosh!' Juliet said again, watching it coming lower and lower. Ropes were thrown out of the basket and secured by six men on the ground. Then the people and the dog stepped out, and a few minutes later Juliet and Monsieur Vapp stepped in. Other people stepped in also.

'*C'est formidable!*' one of them cried, a pretty girl in a hat with flowers on it.

Up and up they went, and then they went sideways over the town. You could see the streets neatly laid out, some of them so straight they looked as if they'd been ruled, others twisting and turning. You could see the harbour and all the yachts and fishing boats, and the roof of Café Le Zeff, and the square, and children playing in the park. You could see the hotel and the place among the white rocks where it was best to bathe, and the sea stretching away for miles, as blue as the sky that was all around when you looked upwards. A couple of seagulls flew quite close to the basket.

'Gosh!' Juliet said again.

'It's a long way to Tipperary!' Monsieur Vapp shouted above the rushing noise. 'Eh, Juliet?'

Juliet laughed. She knew he'd say it again. He'd been waiting for a special occasion.

'Yes, it is,' she shouted back, and just then the flowery hat was blown off the pretty girl's head and went swooping slowly down, round and round in a circle as if it wasn't at all in a hurry to reach the ground.

'Oh, *là, là!*' cried the pretty girl, and she leaned out over the edge of the basket to see where her hat was going to land. But soon it was no bigger than a dot, and then you could hardly see it at all. The man she was with put his arm around her.

Being up in the air was quite like being in the sea. Birds probably felt quite like fish, Juliet thought, floating around in all that space. Then she remembered the eight trout in the fish-tank, and shivered when she thought of them bumping into the glass sides whenever they tried to exercise their gills. Being in a tank was the very opposite of being up in the air, with the wind blowing and feeling as free as a bird, and she wondered if birds in cages were ever brought into a dining-room so that people could choose one. Even at this very moment the waiters would be laying the tables, and the little eyes of the smallest trout would be watching the fish knives and forks being put in place and the pink napkins arranged in their special dining-room shapes, and salt and pepper put on all the tables. Juliet couldn't think of a more sorrowful place in all the world than the fish-tank, except perhaps a bird-cage in some other dining-room. And here she was herself, having the time of her life in a balloon basket!

'It isn't fair,' Juliet whispered. '*Poor* little pets!'

The balloon began to float downwards and when it landed it was at a different balloon station. A bus took the people who'd been on the trip back into the town.

'Not a word to your Grandmamma,' Monsieur Vapp said, winking at Juliet and giving her a fifty-franc note as they stepped off the bus in the square. 'I hope she won't feel neglected,' he said to himself, but Juliet just managed to hear. He hurried away, leaving Juliet to dawdle back to the hotel on her own.

'It isn't fair,' she said again, and some passers-by in swimsuits looked at her and laughed. Juliet didn't mind. She kept remembering the wind blowing into her face and her hair, and the seagulls going by. It was then that she decided what she'd better do. And although she didn't know it at the time, it was then that Juliet's own story began.

That night, when her Grandmamma and Monsieur Vapp were having their cognac in the bar and Juliet was meant to be asleep, she got up and put her clothes on. She crept downstairs and made for the dining-room.

It was practically in darkness. The waiters had set the tables for breakfast, taking away all the cutlery that was necessary for dinner. The only light came from the trout-tank.

Still no one had selected the smallest trout.

'Pet,' Juliet whispered. '*Dear* little pet!'

She counted the others: there were now only five fish in the tank, including the smallest one. She tiptoed across the dining-room to the door that the waiters came through with their trays of food, and returned through with piles of plates. Two lights were burning in the kitchen, one above a row of sinks, the other over a row of gas stoves. Juliet had never seen such an enormous kitchen before. A table filled the centre of it, and there were surfaces for working on around all the walls. Higher up on the walls there were cupboards. There weren't any chairs.

In one corner there was a stack of red plastic buckets, one inside another. Juliet took one up to her room.

CHAPTER 7

'*Bonjour, Mademoiselle,*' the little man with the toys greeted Juliet the next morning. Then he remembered and spoke in English. 'See, I keep the pig for you. I put to one side.'

Juliet shook her head. Not the pig, she explained. It was the fish he'd said he'd put on one side.

'Ah, so. The fish.'

And there it was, squirming and wriggling on the palm of his hand.

'You buy? Hours of pleasure he give.'

'I need five.'

'Five? Oh, *là, là!*'

He searched in his big blue box. He produced two more, and then a third and a fourth. He shook his head.

'Is all,' he said.

'I need five.'

'Then I must make one more.'

'You *make* the fish?' Juliet was astonished because naturally she'd imagined the real-looking fish must be made in a factory.

'*Mais oui*. I make the fish. I make the crocodile. And the pig. And the hen. And the cow and the snake. Everything I make.'

'How long would it take to make a fish? We are going home tomorrow.'

'A half-hour.'

'Gosh!'

Already the toyseller was packing away his toys. He slung the big blue box over his shoulder.

'Are you sure you have some money? Kind father or mother . . . ?'

Juliet showed him the fifty-franc note Monsieur Vapp had given her. To her dismay he shook his head again. He slipped the box off his shoulder and placed it on the quayside again.

'For five fish, sixty francs.'

'I haven't got sixty francs.'

'For four fish, forty-eight francs.'

'Oh.'

'Perhaps you ask kind –'

'It would be too late.'

'What you do with five fish?'

So Juliet told him.

'Ha, ha, ha,' laughed the toymaker.

'I can carry the real ones in the bucket down to where we have our swim. I can put them back into the sea.'

'I make you one. Just for the fun of it.'

The blue box was hoisted on to his back again and they set off together. When he'd said 'just for the fun of it,' Juliet was reminded of the gate-girl having as much fun in the garden as the daytime children, so she told the toymaker the story. Then, to pass the time, she told him the story about the sunflowers in the snow, and then the one about witches.

'I think you like stories?'

'Yes, I do.'

'One from Ireland you tell me, one from England, one from Wales. None from poor old Scotland, eh?'

'I don't know one about Scotland.'

Just then Juliet heard her grandmother's voice calling out to her, asking where she thought she was going. When Juliet explained, her grandmother said she intended to accompany her.

'Please, of course,' the toymaker invited with a bow.

His house was a respectable yellow-painted one in a row with others. He led the way into it and then showed Juliet and her grandmother from room to room. One was full of spinning-tops, all of them different colours and all of which played music when they span. The next room was full of animals, and in the next one was a huge doll's house that reached to the ceiling.

'Gosh!' Juliet exclaimed. '*Gosh!*'

But the toymaker said he had a living to make and led his visitors to his workshop, where half-completed toys were scattered all over the workbenches and there were shelves with different coloured paint in pots, and cog-wheels and pieces of tin hanging on nails, and springs for making the toys go, and keys for winding them up.

'*I* know one about Scotland,' the toymaker said, taking a piece of tin and marking the outline of a fish on it. 'The time I was in Scotland I learn this story.'

He told Juliet about the great battles of long ago, when kings rode out on horses, and queens were forever doing needlework. He said there was a particular King of Scotland who hated the battles. As well as that, he hated various sports that were popular – especially throwing trees about. This particular king much preferred to remain in his castle warming himself by the fire or strolling in his gardens. His queen, on the other hand, was bored by the fire and detested the gardens, and always got her stitches wrong when she picked up an embroidery.

'Oh, how I should love to go riding into battle!' she used to cry, staring out from the battlements in search of enemies who might be planning an attack. When *he* thought of an attack, and of his great armies of soldiers arriving at his castle so that he could lead them, the king felt jittery in his stomach.

'Banging about with a sword!' the queen used to cry. 'Oh me, oh my, just think of it!'

Every time she said that the king would look up from her embroidery and give a little shudder. He was very clever with her embroidery and could get it right for her in a matter of seconds.

One day, when the soldiers demanded to be led because there was trouble somewhere, the king confided to his queen that he was feeling a trifle unwell. He was certain it would do him no good whatsoever to go rampaging about the countryside in his kilt and helmet. The queen, who was very fond of him, said: 'Just you lie down awhile, dear. I'll order up tea and fresh hot oatcakes. Only lock

He was sitting up in bed, humming an old Scottish air.

the bedroom door and on no account speak to anyone or let anyone see you.'

So the queen put on the king's kilt and his helmet and all the rest of his kingly protection, and strapped on his sword, and took his spurs down from the mantelpiece where he kept them. She pulled down the visor of the helmet so that her face would not be seen. In the kitchen of the castle she ordered that a tray of weak tea and oatcakes should be sent up to the queen and left outside the royal bedroom door. She'd be away for an hour or two, she said, engaging in battle.

While she was gone the king finished the embroidery she had begun, unstitching most of it because she'd made a terrible mess of it. He began another one, of peacocks in a tree. He was sitting up in bed, humming an old Scottish air, when he heard the queen's tap on the door.

'I'm back, dear,' she called out in a strong, gruff voice, just in case a servant was listening, and then she clanked in, covered in blood and delighted with herself.

The king bathed her wounds and dressed them and then gently put her to bed. He sent the helmet and armour downstairs for a good scrubbing. She'd won the battle of course, and the next day hundreds of thanes and chieftains arrived at the castle to say thank you.

'Oh, it was nothing,' the king said.

After that, five princes and five princesses were born to the king and queen, and in between times whenever there was a battle the queen rode out and the king went to bed.

'I'm a King Who Married the Right Queen,' the king said.

'And I married the right king,' the queen delightedly replied. And in all the long history of kings and queens in Scotland, or anywhere else come to that, no two royal personages were as happy. No one found out, not even the royal children, that the queen who was famous for her embroideries had never been able to get her stitches right.

'The end,' said the toymaker.

During the telling of the story Juliet had been so engrossed that she'd hardly noticed what he was doing with his pieces of tin and his cog-wheels and his springs. When she looked there was another fish in his hand and he was winding it up to see if it worked.

'Perfect,' he said when it flapped and wriggled on his palm. 'Now all we need is the paint.'

In no time at all he had painted eyes on the fish, and painted its tummy a silvery white and speckled its back in a lifelike way, and drawn in its mouth with a fine brush. 'Four minutes to dry,' he said, placing the completed fish in a drying oven. 'We French are an efficient people,' he added, winking at Juliet and her grandmother.

'More likely you're a genius,' Juliet said politely. 'And what a lovely house you have!'

'I travel everywhere selling the toys. I put the shutters up and am very sad because I love the little house. But you have to make a living.'

They walked back to the quays with the new fish added to the four in the blue box. Juliet's Grandmamma went to join Monsieur Vapp, and the toymaker opened the box and put the five fish in a bag.

'Ha, ha, ha.' He laughed again, and then again. 'Ha, ha, ha,' he laughed. 'I'd love to see their faces.'

Juliet held out the fifty-franc note, but to her great surprise the toymaker shook his head. It was too good a joke, he said. No one should take money for a joke.

'But you have to make a living.'

'Better to make a joke than a living.'

'But –'

'*Mais non*. No more buts.' And the toymaker spun one of his tops, the one that played the bagpipes.

'You are the nicest man in France,' Juliet said, shouting above the music.

'I know I am,' the toymaker solemnly agreed.

'Oh, *là, là!*' exclaimed Monsieur Vapp when he tried to put his fork into the trout he'd ordered.

It went flying across the dining-room, ending up in a dish of fruit salad.

When the woman in purple tried to cut the head off hers, it flew up in the air and broke a light bulb.

The very thin couple banged at their trout with the handles of their knives to show the waiter that something was the matter.

The sad man held his up by the tail in order to examine it.

Other people in the restaurant laughed, and Monsieur Vapp laughed too. The waiters were beside themselves. The manager scuttled round the tables, saying there'd been some mistake.

'Bring me some steak,' ordered Monsieur Vapp, and Juliet thought of the smallest trout, and the four others she'd rescued, swimming about at the bottom of the sea, among the shells and the rocks.

'So that's what it was all about,' Juliet's Grand-mamma exclaimed. 'What an amusement!'

Tomorrow night, the manager promised every-one, there would be real trout back in the fish-tank, a fine choice, the best in France.

At least she wouldn't have to see them, Juliet thought. She began to laugh and couldn't stop. She made her hand into a fist and pressed it against her mouth, but it didn't do any good. She wished Kitty Ann were there. She wished Kitty Ann could have seen the face of the woman in purple, and the sad man holding up his trout by the tail.

'Drink some water,' her Grandmamma ordered, but when Juliet tried to she spluttered the water all over the place, which made her laugh even more. Everyone in the dining-room was looking at her, but she still couldn't stop. The chef was standing in the doorway to the kitchen, laughing his head off, and Juliet guessed he'd known what he was doing when he fried the mechanical fish.

'I think we know who has a story of her own now,' Juliet's grandmother said.

CHAPTER 8

On the way back to County Tipperary Juliet retold the story of the King Who Married the Right Queen. Her grandmother listened, but Juliet could see she was preoccupied.

'Miles away,' her grandmother confessed. 'Sorry, dear.'

When they arrived in London they were met by the polite man, who was just the same except that this time his scarf and tie were green, with dots. He carried their suitcases, which were heavier than before because they were full of presents from France. He saw them safely into the train and then lingered to have a private word with Juliet's grandmother.

'Dear man, I don't know!' Juliet heard her Grandmamma whispering. Her Grandmamma kissed the polite man on the cheek and promised to write him a letter.

When they reached Dublin the teasing man with the moustache met them off the boat and drove them across the city to the station. He, too, had a private moment with Juliet's grandmother. He, too, was kissed on the cheek.

'First thing I do when Juliet's delivered,' Juliet's Grandmamma promised, 'is to write you a letter.'

On the train the same ticket collector punched their tickets and said the weather wasn't as good as it might be.

'Still and all,' he said, 'a drop of rain won't hurt the sweetpeas.'

'I wonder if those people will ever choose trout again,' Juliet remarked to her Grandmamma, trying to cheer her up because she'd gone quiet again.

'What's that, dear?'

But when Juliet repeated what she'd said her Grandmamma only shook her head as if she still hadn't heard properly.

'They all want to marry me,' she eventually revealed. 'Did you ever hear of such a thing!'

Monsieur Vapp and the polite man and the teasing man all wanted to marry her, and she asked Juliet what she thought.

'None of them,' Juliet advised her. 'Not that they aren't very nice,' she quickly added. 'I'd marry the toymaker.'

'But unfortunately, dear, I didn't really get to know him.'

'We were always passing him on the quay.'

'I know, dear, but Monsieur Vapp was always talking.'

'You could write him a letter.'

But her Grandmamma shook her head. It would be difficult to know how to begin a letter to a man she didn't know. She sighed as the train hurried them through meadows and woods, past farmhouses and ruins and hills with sheep on them, and then over the flat boglands that Juliet remembered from their other journey, and then into the mountains. She didn't know what to do, her Grandmamma kept saying.

'It'll be something to think about,' Juliet reminded her, trying to be helpful.

'It'll be that all right.'

Suddenly her Grandmamma said she'd like the teasing man and the polite man and Monsieur Vapp to be their secret. Not a word to Juliet's mother and father, she requested, just in case they considered the whole thing unduly amusing. So Juliet promised.

'It's a pity you couldn't try them out,' she suggested.

'I'm afraid they wouldn't agree to that.'

'The toymaker would. You could tell just to look at him. But then you wouldn't have to try him out because you'd definitely have fallen in love with him. Anyone would.'

'Ah, well.'

Juliet's father was there at the station. He hugged Juliet and said he'd missed her like nobody's business. There was a surprise for her, he added casually, back at the house.

The surprise would be a puppy, Juliet thought. At last they had taken notice of the hints she had been dropping, about how a puppy would complete the family. But it wasn't a puppy. The surprise was a plump little baby in a pram.

'Give him a cuddle,' Juliet's mother invited, smiling at Juliet's surprise. 'Only be very careful.'

So Juliet gave her brother a cuddle. She held him in her arms and said he was lovely. 'The best baby in County Tipperary,' her father proudly corrected her.

'Better than a puppy,' Juliet agreed. 'Aren't you, pet?'

Her brother made a gurgling sound, and smiled even though he hadn't any teeth to smile with. 'Oh, *là, là!'* Juliet murmured, and then she ran out into the town to see how everything was.

Nothing had changed. She read the inscription on the 1798 Memorial and the statement above P.J. Kelly's hotel: *P.J. Kelly, licensed to sell tobacco and intoxicating liquors.* She looked over the wall at the crooked grave-stones in the old graveyard, and then climbed up steep Castle Hill to the ruins, and ran down to the poor part of the town to Paddy Old's cottage. She knew by now that he wouldn't have wanted her to go moping about the place, the way she had at first. He hadn't felt sorry for himself in this small cottage that had weeds growing out of the roof. He hadn't felt sorry for himself all the years he had tramped the roads. Having stories to tell made all the difference.

Juliet hurried back through the town to Macnamara's Provisions and Bar and asked Mrs Macnamara if Kitty Ann was upstairs.

'She is of course,' Mrs Macnamara said. 'How're you doing, Juliet?'

'All right,' Juliet said, running through the back of the shop and up the stairs.

'Will you look what the cat's brought in!' Kitty Ann almost screamed. 'The blooming wanderer returned!'

They went out together, with Madra tagging

along behind them, down to Dandelion Meadow. Kitty Ann said she knew about Juliet's brother, had even held him in her arms.

'What else happened?' Juliet asked.

'Sister Catherine had a tooth out. Miss Walsh is getting married.'

'Who to?'

'Foley in Phelan's. I only hope she knows what she's doing.'

'Is the Russian Princess all right?'

Kitty Ann said she was, and then Juliet told her everything that had happened, how three different men had wanted to marry her grandmother, how she'd gone up in a balloon basket, how the toymaker had helped her to get the fish back into the sea.

'It's great you're home again,' Kitty Ann said, but she sounded a little forlorn.

Juliet knew Kitty Ann was envious so she said it would all have been better if she had been there as well. And because Kitty Ann didn't like stories as much as she did she didn't tell her about the Sunflowers in the Snow or the Weekend Witch or the Gate-girl and the Snail. She saved those up, with the King Who Married the Right Queen, to tell her brother when he was old enough; and if he didn't want to listen it wouldn't matter because one day she would write the stories down and anyone who wanted to could read them.

Juliet knew now – but didn't know how she knew – that wherever there were other stories she would find them and write them down also. They would come to her in dreams and in real events that happened and in things people said. She would change bits of them and add bits to them because that was what you had to do, making them your own.

Stories made the world go round, Juliet said to herself, while Kitty Ann chattered on and they lay in the long grass in the evening sunshine.

KATE THOMPSON

THE Switchers TRILOGY

'Kate Thompson writes with
a marvellous and magical ease.' TES

*Kate Thompson's Switchers trilogy
is riveting reading. Once you have
begun, you will never want to stop.*

Switchers
Tess is a Switcher - she can change shape to
become any animal she chooses. She always
thought she was unique, but not any more. Tess meets another
Switcher, Kevin, and together they have powers they never
dreamed of.

Midnight's Choice *Switchers 2*
Tess senses a call which is at once welcoming and terrifying, too.
Will she choose the path of darkness…?

Wild Blood *Switchers 3*
With her fifteenth birthday imminent, Tess is running out of time
to decide who, or what, she will become when she switches for the
last time. What on earth will she do in the wilds of the woods?
And what will the wild woods do to her?

OUT NOW IN PAPERBACK FROM RED FOX AT £4.99

ONLY HUMAN

Kate Thompson

The second book in The Missing Link trilogy

Whatever it was that had caught him was heading straight down for the deep. Although he didn't have a dolphin's sonar system, Danny had a strong sixth sense that helped him to orient himself in the darkness of the sea and identify other living things. He had encountered all sorts of weird and wonderful creatures in the deep, but the one that was dragging him now was something outside his experience.

About a hundred metres down, Danny's captor levelled off and began to swim parallel to the surface, away from *The Privateer*. Now Danny could feel the powerful beating of fins creating turbulence in the water beside his head. His panic was depriving him of oxygen, and he began to fear that he would drown before this creature, whatever it was, ever got around to eating him. With a tremendous effort, he bent double and managed to reach his ankle. But what his fingers encountered there sent a swift shock through his blood.

There was no mouth, no teeth, no predator's jaw. The thing that gripped him felt much more like a human hand.

Now available from The Bodley Head at £10.99

ISBN 0370326636

the BEGUILERS

KATE THOMPSON

'You calm down, young lady,
or it's off after beguilers
you'll be.' Maybe my mother
shouldn't have said that.
Maybe it put the idea into
my head.

Every night they came drifting through the village
streets, issuing their mournful cries, terrorizing the
population. It wasn't safe to go out after dark.
Everyone knew the power of the beguilers.

No one knew what they were. No one had ever caught
one. But every generation threw up a beguiler hunter;
a tragic soul considered by the rest of the villagers
to be insane.

Rilka knows she isn't mad. But the desire to catch a
beguiler is about to change her life, and the lives of
those around her, for ever.

Out now in Hardback from The Bodley Head.
ISBN 0370325737   £10.99

THE WOLVES OF WILLOUGHBY CHASE

JOAN AIKEN

*She woke suddenly to find that the train had stopped with a jerk.
'Oh! What is it? Where are we?' she exclaimed before she could stop herself.
'No need to alarm yourself, miss,' said her companion. 'Wolves on the line,
most likely – they often have trouble of that kind hereabouts.'
'Wolves!' Sylvia stared at him in terror.*

After braving a treacherous journey through snow-covered wastes
populated by packs of wild and hungry wolves, Sylvia joins her cousin
Bonnie in the warmth and safety of Willoughby Chase. But with
Bonnie's parents overseas and the evil Miss Slighcarp left in charge, the
cousins soon find their human predators even harder to escape.

'Joan Aiken is such a spellbinder that it all rings true...'
THE STANDARD

ISBN 0099411865   £4.99

THE
TOWER
ROOM
BY
ADÈLE GERAS

'I'm going to kiss you,' he said. 'If you don't mind, that is.' I couldn't speak. I just closed my eyes and waited. He kissed me very softly on the lips, so that I could hardly feel it, but I smelled his smell in my nostrils, and his hands were on my shoulders. I opened my eyes.

Megan, Bella and Alice survey the drama of everyday life from the Tower Room of their isolated boarding school, Egerton Hall. As their schooldays draw to an end they are already sensing the dangerous delights awaiting them in the outside world. But as Megan looks down one unforgettable morning and meets Simon's inquisitive gaze, her safe, cocooned world is soon transformed forever.

The Egerton Hall Trilogy:
The Tower Room **ISBN 0099409542**   **£4.99**
Watching the Roses ISBN 0099417235   £4.99
Pictures of the Night ISBN 0099409739   £4.99